OUTCAST

A MONTAGUE & STRONG DETECTIVE AGENCY NOVEL
BOOK 24

ORLANDO A. SANCHEZ

ABOUT THE STORY

Forsaken. Feared. Forgotten.

When the Grand Council Emissary officially sanctions the Montague and Strong Detective Agency, with Monty and Simon officially declared magus non grata—rogue mages, their world is shattered, figuratively and literally.

Haven, The NYTF, the Dark Council, all of the mage sects and neutral locations worldwide have been instructed to treat them as outcasts.

Anyone assisting them in any way will suffer the most extreme of consequences—erasure and death.

Now, with the help of the Ten, Monty and Simon must confront the Emissary of the Grand Council and his schemes.

They will discover that being outcasts doesn't mean being alone. It means that when everything is at its darkest, some will still stand by you, shining the light of defiance.

"Standing alone doesn't mean you are alone.
It means you are strong enough to handle things all by yourself."

DEDICATION

To the forgotten, forsaken and unloved.
You are not alone as long as one person holds a light for you,
and if you cannot find that person—become that person.

ONE

I stared at Monty and shook my head.

We were standing near the entrance of a specially designed obstacle-labyrinth course. Dexter had created it to train the potential battlemages he planned to torture, once the Montague School of Battlemagic was operational.

"I can appreciate the work Dex put into this course," I said, glancing at the entrance. "I don't see why I'm being chosen to break it in, you know not being a mage and all that."

"Precisely," Monty said. "The Cretan Course was designed for fledgling mages embarking on the battlemage path."

"You just made my argument for me," I said, shooting him a glare. "I'm not a fledgling mage embarking on *any* path."

"You're not a proficient mage, yet," he said. "There's still some hope for you. Right now you're in the same position of students who will be using and training on this course. I'd say you're a perfect candidate."

"Feels more like the perfect guinea pig."

"Are you insinuating I'm trying out new, untested devices,

traps, and casts on an unsuspecting target?" he asked. "That seems a bit extreme. I think you may be overreacting."

"Overreacting?" I took a deep breath. It's possible I was overreacting, but I had a good reason for it. I was being hunted by my own hellhound. "I'm not *insinuating* anything. You *are* trying out new, untested devices, traps, and casts on an unsuspecting target—me."

Peaches rumbled at me as Monty produced a sausage and fed it to my ever voracious hellhound, who proceeded to hoover it out of sight instantly. I wasn't a fan of this arrangement they had. Monty would create sausages out of thin air, in return, Peaches would chase me through the torture maze as fast as he could.

I knew for a fact Peaches was enjoying himself because he told me as much. He could move faster than was fair.

<*I can't believe you would agree to this. I'm your bondmate.*>

<*The angry man makes good meat. He said he would make extra meat if I caught you fast. I like extra meat.*>

<*I'm your bondmate. Don't you think this is wrong?*>

<*Meat is never wrong. Extra meat is good for me. I'm still growing. You should eat extra meat, then you could grow too.*>

<*Extra meat is good, except when it's poisoned. Remember Thomas?*>

<*He was a bad man. The angry man makes good meat and he gives me extra. You are still my bondmate. You are always my bondmate. Would you like some of my meat?*>

<*I would like you not to chase me through this maze.*>

<*Then I don't get meat. Meat is life. I will give you some of my meat, then you will run faster. That will make catching you harder.*>

<*I doubt even you believe that. This is bondmate abuse, you know.*>

<*I would never abuse you. You are the best bondmate I know. Do you feel better now?*>

<*I'm the only bondmate you know.*>

I shook my head.

My own hellhound selling me out for spectacular meat made sense, but it didn't mean I had to like it. I, also knew Peaches was only doing this because this was training, and Monty was making the meat. He would never betray me if this was a real-life scenario.

The image of the two of us, bloody and beaten, facing off against a horde of Shadowhounds and shamblers was still fresh in my memory.

Kali's words came back to me from that nightmare scenario—a true nightmare scenario and I would do everything in my power to prevent it from happening.

"It looks grim, does it not?"

"It looks like death."

"Yes, in this situation, my curse would keep you alive, but your hellhound would perish. He is not immortal. Nigh indestructible, yes, but even hellhounds have their limits. In addition, to save your life, he would sacrifice his own."

"No."

"Yes it's what bondmates do."

"I wouldn't let him."

"There would be no choice."

I shuddered the memory away as I turned to face Monty.

"I don't think this is going to work," I said, glancing from Monty to my determined hellhound. "How am I supposed to outrun a hellhound? He doesn't even run. He blinks in and out as he chases me. That's not running, that's teleporting."

"Consider this good practice," he said. "The next time we encounter a teleporting enemy bent on your destruction, you'll be prepared. Forewarned is forearmed."

"That's not telling me *how* to deal with this theoretical teleporting enemy," I shot back. "All this does is let me know I can't outrun a teleporting enemy."

"The *how* is not my concern," Monty said, looking at his

watch and adjusting one of the dials. It was a recent, dark-blue Patek Philippe Grand Complications acquisition and I could tell he was pleased to show it off, considering his last one had been obliterated. "I just care about the end result."

"The part where I get mangled and slobbered to death?"

"Only if you're slow," he said without looking up from his watch. "Don't be slow."

"You do realize he *can* teleport?" I repeated for emphasis. "How am I supposed to compete with a teleporting hellhound?"

Monty brushed some lint from his sleeve.

"These questions are beginning to sound like excuses," he said. "You *do* realize hellhounds have unnatural enemies?"

I felt a cold shiver grip me briefly.

The unnatural enemies he was mentioning were Shadowhounds.

I thought back to the time I tried to get Peaches obedience lessons with Mori. That hadn't turned out to be such a great idea. We had entered Ezra's training area unarmed—well not that we had a choice.

It was part of Ezra's rules.

No weapons in the training area. At the time, I didn't give it much thought. It seemed like the prudent thing to do. I mean who brings weapons to a training lesson?

Turns out, that when it's a training lesson for a hellhound, I should bring *all* the weapons. Before I knew what was happening, we were facing what I later discovered to be Shadowhounds. Unpleasant creatures about twice the size of a wolf, with poisonous fangs and claws.

Looking to sink them into my hellhound.

The Shadowhounds were specifically created by Hades to destroy hellhounds, and like them, they had the same teleportation ability along with a nasty temperament leaning toward the lethal end of the spectrum.

Even though I had taken Peaches for a training lesson, *I* was really the one being tested. No one bothered to inform me of this little detail until after the lesson was over.

Welcome to my life.

Ezra had wanted to know if I would be able to rise to the occasion. With Mori's help, we managed to fight off several Shadowhounds, and survive the training lesson.

"I'm not seeing what Shadowhounds have to do with me outrunning my hellhound."

"Truly, there are times your mind resembles a neutron star."

"Bright?"

"Dense."

"I thought they flashed? Aren't they called palpitating stars?"

"No, you mean pulsars."

"Exactly. I just said that—flashing stars like a heartbeat, palpitars," I said, secure in the knowledge that this would completely derail the conversation. "Tell me that's not the name of a star."

"It's not, and stop stalling," he said. "You can do this. It's *your* hellhound bondmate. You have nothing to fear. Perhaps some minor mangling, excessive slobber, and a few minor injuries here and there."

I gave my hellhound a wary look. He was practically vibrating with anticipation of our next run.

"He seems too excited to hunt me down."

"He's playing," Monty said, glancing down at Peaches and patting him on the head. "This is good for him as well."

"Good for him?" I asked incredulously. "He cracked one of my ribs with that massive head of his in a battering-ram move. Then he dislocated one of my shoulders when he blinked out and reappeared above me, right before landing on me with all of his weight."

Monty nodded.

"That *was* quite creative," he said. "I'd say his mastery of teleportation has increased considerably. We will have to find new ways to challenge him and test the limits of his abilities."

"That wreckage was just on the last run. That's your idea of fun?"

"For me? No. For him? I'm sure he's enjoying himself immensely."

"You know what? We should take a break," I said, holding up a hand. "How about two, three, months from now, we meet up again for another try of 'Simon gets mangled'?"

"You are improving," Monty said. "Last time you almost lasted three minutes. You need more focus. Perhaps employ some feints and misdirection in your strategy?"

"More focus?" I said, looking at him in disbelief. "You seriously think I'm failing because I lack focus?"

"That and I think you need to take this seriously," he answered. "This is not only training for you. Your pup needs to go through these training courses. Since you never procured formal lessons for him, this will have to suffice as a replacement."

I stared at him for a good three seconds.

"The last two attempts say otherwise," I said. "Also aside from teleporting, he has twice as many legs as I do. He weighs about as much as the Dark Goat and knows how to use his weight as a weapon. This is completely unfair."

"Simon, you, like your creature, have grown in ability and skill," he said, staring at me. "Commensurate with that growth, our enemies have also grown in threat level. If you do not learn to do this when some creature isn't trying to rip off your arms and bludgeon you to death with them, you will be forced to learn how to deal with these threats *in situ*. That is *not* ideal."

"I know it's not," I snapped. "I have yet to meet an ogre

willing to take a moment to let me blast it comfortably. All of my learning has been *in situ*. What did you expect? We're constantly up against some insane creature trying to turn us into paste."

"Which I'm trying to mitigate with this exercise," Monty finished. "These simulations have value. Now if you're done stalling, let's run it again. This time be creative, use misdirection, and really try to hit him this time."

"You want me to really hit my hellhound?" I asked concerned. "I don't want to hurt him."

"Hurt him?" he asked, looking at me, then at Peaches. "Your hellhound has been hit by vehicles and beings far larger and more dangerous than you, with the intent to cause him real harm, and he walked away with no lasting harm. I don't think you can actually hurt him at this stage in his growth."

"That and he's not even giving me a chance to react to his attacks."

"That too," he said with a nod. "Perhaps pickup the pace, think a few steps ahead and try to actually outwit him. Be proactive, not reactive."

"Why do I get the feeling you're enjoying this too?"

"I have no idea what you're talking about," Monty said, waving my words away. "I do this strictly for the data. I take no pleasure from seeing your hellhound land on you in a single bound, nearly crushing you into oblivion. What kind of person do you take me for, some kind of sadist?"

"I think you're the kind of mage that would enjoy seeing me crushed repeatedly," I said, taking my place at the start of the obstacle-labyrinth course. Monty crouched down and whispered something in my hellhound's ear. "What exactly are you telling him?"

"Nothing significant," Monty said, waving my words away as Peaches took his place several feet behind me. "I promised him extra, extra meat if he managed to stop you in under a minute. So far he has excelled in your apprehension and detention, but it's still too slow. He needs to move faster."

"You what?" I asked, incredulous. "Did you just tell him to move…faster?"

"Ready?" Monty asked. "Remember, no providing contrary instruction. This training needs to be as authentic as possible."

"If it's supposed to be authentic, why am *I* the only one being chased in this simulation?" I asked. "Why isn't my lovely hellhound chasing and pouncing all over the *both* of us?"

"First of all," he said, pointing to his suit, "this is a recently runed bespoke Zegna; it doesn't take hellhound slobber well. In addition, your hellhound has been known to destroy my property. This is a brand new Patek." He held up his wrist to show me his amazing watch—I mean timepiece. "I was on the waiting list forever before they agreed to my purchase."

"I'm sure the next creature we face will respect your love of overpriced watches," I said. "I'm sure they'll be careful not to crush your wrist along with the watch."

"First, timepiece not, watch," he corrected and continued. "What you wear is a watch. Second, and more importantly, out of the three of us here, only one of us lacks the ability to teleport away from danger. Care to guess who?"

"Oh, ha, ha," I said, shaking out my arms and looking ahead at the training course Dex had created at the school. "I still think this is unfair."

"Duly noted," he said with a nod. "I'll even make sure you get a five second head start."

"Your generosity knows no limits," I said. "A whole five seconds? Truly, I'm touched."

"It has been mentioned more than once. Ready?"

I nodded.

He raised an arm and brought it down.

"And...go!"

I ran into the obstacle.

Even if I could really hit Peaches—which I couldn't—he was my hellhound after all; there was nothing I could hit him with hard enough to throw him off course.

He was basically a tank disguised as a hellhound.

His skin had been getting denser lately, especially after he had entered battleform a few times. It was as if his skin retained some of the properties of the battleform even when he was no longer in it.

I headed into a corridor, mentally ticking off the seconds. Monty would be fair in that he would hold Peaches for an actual five seconds, then he would unleash him on me.

If this had been a real scenario, fear would be my driving motivator. There was nothing quite like having a hellhound chasing you. Right after the fear, despair would settle in as I realized that it was pointless.

There was no way to escape a determined hellhound coming after you. I couldn't even hear him. For such a large animal, Peaches was incredibly quiet.

The only thing that saved me was our bond. I could sense him when he approached and blinked. Every blink felt like he disappeared from my senses. When he blinked back in, his presence would rush at my senses.

Usually by then, it was too late and he was above me or right on me, but I was getting better at telling where he was.

It took me a few seconds, and three runs to realize that I was failing because, aside from the fact that I was up against a *hellhound*, I was playing by the rules.

No more rules.

I formed a dawnward and focused my energy, waiting some distance from the corner of an intersection in the labyrinth. With the right angle, my dawnward could obscure his vision and I would be able to land a shot on Peaches with my magic missile.

He wanted to play hardball, we were going to play hardball.

Even so, I would make it a glancing blow. I knew he was tough, but my magic missile really packed a punch.

I didn't want to hurt him—not even accidentally.

I crouched down near the curvature of the dawnward and waited. I heard his paws on the stone of the obstacle course and I knew he wasn't even bothering to hide.

He knew where I was and he was coming for me.

I was ready.

TWO

I only thought I was ready.

I kept my focus, and let my senses expand. My hellhound was approaching my location, getting closer by the second. When he was several dozen feet away, I sensed him blink out and blink back in. He reappeared twenty feet behind me with a low growl.

I was certain he felt, like the last two times, that he had me.

"*Ignisvitae*," I whispered under my breath as I turned, unleashing a column of flame which leaped from my hand and raced at him. "Game over, boy."

I didn't pour too much power into the magic missile. I wasn't trying to hurt him, just stun him long enough to get away from his impending slobber and pouncing attack.

Rather than leap or teleport away, Peaches kept advancing on my position. The flame kept closing in on him and still, he ran at me.

I moved back and watched in horror as the column of flame enveloped his body. He howled in pain for a few seconds as the flame engulfed him.

"No," I said shocked as I stopped moving, frozen in disbelief. I swore he would've dodged out of the way. "Peaches!"

He took a few steps toward me, let his tongue loll to one side of his mouth, and proceeded to fall on his side with a loud *thump*. There was still smoke wafting up from his body as he crashed into the ground.

I couldn't believe I really managed to hit him.

He had never let me hit him in the previous runs. I saw his body lying still and I feared the worst.

How could this have happened?

I rushed over to his side and crouched down to check his body for damage and burns, all thoughts of the obstacle course and training gone from my mind.

As I gently felt his body, I heard him breathe a raspy, wheezy sound.

<Bondmate, come closer.>

I leaned in closer to him.

"I'm sorry, boy," I said as I rubbed his side and worry filled me. "I didn't mean to—"

His sudden movement caught me by surprise. I moved back, off-balance as he quickly rolled to his feet, took about three steps and jumped into the air.

He disappeared from view for about a second. I immediately made to get to my feet, but it was too late. I had fallen for his trap. He reappeared above me and came crashing down directly on my chest.

The air escaped my lungs with a *whoosh* as he sat on me and held me in place. I gasped for air and rolled to the side, shoving him to one side as I tried to make my escape.

He barely budged, but I managed to get my legs free and attempted to shove him off with a hip push.

My hip push barely moved him. He slapped me across the face with his wet tongue and blinded me with hellhound slobber.

"Ugh," I said trying to wipe the slobber from my eyes. "No fair!"

<Frank says everything is fair in meat and war.>

<It's love and war, and Frank is going to get a serious stomping when I see him next. Was he the one who taught you that trick?>

<Yes, look weak when you are strong. He said I needed to learn to faint. So I fainted.>

<I think the lizard meant feint. Either way, you got me good. You can get off now. You're not exactly light you know, and you're crushing my lungs.>

<You cannot escape. The angry man promised me extra meat for holding you still.>

<You can't hold me still.>

I turned and shoved him away. He slid across the ground for all of ten inches. It wasn't much, but it gave me a small gap of space.

It was all I needed.

I rolled to my feet and unleashed a magic missile to his face. He rumbled a low growl and shook his massive head as he bounced back a few feet. He rumbled again, turning to get me in his sights. That's when I saw the runes on his flanks light up a bright red.

"You can't be serious," I said, pointing at him. "Don't you dare. You're going to use a—?"

Twin beams of power exploded from his eyes, headed for my chest. I dove to the side as his baleful glare scored the wall behind me, digging out a deep trench in the stone.

I whirled on him, ready to yell about the use of excessive force, but he was already gone.

I started running.

I had an idea.

I knew what he would try. In all our battles together I learned that he did have some predictable moves. He would try to ram me into next week as I tried to get away.

When I felt him close, I dove forward, causing him to miss crashing into me. I scrambled to my feet and made it to one of the closest intersections, taking a sharp left and shaking him. I heard him slam into a wall behind me as he tried to stop me—then silence.

That was not good.

I kept running, preparing another magic missile.

I turned a corner and too late, I sensed him.

"*Ignis*—oof, was all I managed before he caught up to me.

A hellhound-shaped freight train crashed into my side, knocking all the air from my lungs and launching me forward. He blinked out and reappeared a few feet ahead before clamping his massive jaws around one of my arms.

The immediate change in weight brought me crashing down to the ground. We rolled for several feet and ended up in a tangled mess. Throughout our tumble, he never released his hold on my arm.

I scratched his side.

He started to kick a foot and I knew I had triggered an involuntary twitching movement. He loosened his grip on my arm and I pulled my arm away.

"*Ignisvitae*," I said and hit him with another magic missile.

Again it wasn't powerful enough to hurt him, but it hit him hard enough to make a Knocker mage proud. I bounced him down the corridor, buying myself some much-needed time. Enough to use my next attack.

I focused and traced runes I never thought I would use again, forming a large broccoli-laced sausage. I made sure to add extra broccoli to this one.

It was the ultimate Healthy Hellhound Delight.

There was no way I was going to be able to win this fight attacking him from the outside—so I had to fight dirty and attack his only weakness—his stomach.

I hoped I survived the hellhound gas.

He appeared a second later, blinking in to land in front of me. I threw him the sausage, which he proceeded to catch mid-air and inhaled.

I was going to have to train him not to eat every airborne sausage that approached him. I still remember the tactic Thomas used to try and take him out. His stomach really was his weakness.

Once I saw him swallow the sausage, I turned and ran for my life.

I was too late.

THREE

Peaches fell on his side and this time I knew he wasn't faking it.

His stomach started jackhammering and I heard the dreaded, but familiar sound of machine gun fire, reverberating from his stomach.

Turns out, hellhound metabolisms are much faster than I imagined. I heard him growl in discomfort right before the cloud of broccoli-induced deathane engulfed me and squeezed the air from my body in a stranglehold.

How could he digest it so fast?

My vision blurred as my eyes teared up. A burning sensation exploded all over my body, and for a brief moment, I wondered if the miasma that had escaped my hellhound was somehow alive as it tried to choke the life out of me.

Taking short, shallow breaths, I stumbled back to the entrance of the obstacle-labyrinth with a sense of victory. It may not have been dignified, but I had beaten my hellhound.

All is fair in meat and war.

"What did you do?" Monty asked as I exited the course.

He immediately covered his face and took several steps back. "What *is* that stench?"

"*That* is the stench of victory," I said, gasping. "I beat him. You wanted me to be creative, so I created."

"It smells like you created an environmental biohazard."

"Welcome to hellhound deathane," I said trying not to breathe in too deeply. "I wonder if we could weaponize this?"

"The weapon in question is not supposed to eliminate both sides," he said. "It defeats the purpose of utilizing it as a weapon against someone if you obliterate yourself in the process."

"True, gives a new meaning to mutually assured destruction," I said with a nod. "Let's pass on weaponizing hellhound gastric gases."

"Are you *certain* you didn't destroy his digestive system?" he asked as he coughed a few times. I noticed his eyes were watering up and smiled. He deserved this and more for having my hellhound mangle me with the excuse of training. "What did you give him?"

"Healthy Hellhound Delight," I said. "With extra broccoli."

He turned to stare at me.

"You didn't," he said, incredulously. "Are you trying to get us killed?"

"I'm pretty sure the instructions were: be creative, use misdirection, and really try to hit him," I answered, still moving away from the course. "I creatively misdirected my hellhound to eat his favorite food, where I proceeded to really hit him from the inside."

"As creative as that is, it does expose a weakness in his otherwise formidable defenses," Monty said. "Your hellhound *can* be attacked through his stomach. As my burning eyes can attest."

"He may need some major training in that area," I said. "I think we need to pay Hades a visit."

Monty was about to answer when the course was rocked by the sound of gas exiting my hellhound's body with epic force. I looked up and saw my now airborne hellhound fly across the course and crash land a few feet away.

He cratered the ground, creating a large cloud of deathane in his wake as he shook his body and slowly padded over to where I stood.

Monty moved away, quickly giving him plenty of space.

Peaches rubbed his enormous head on my leg and nearly knocked me to the ground in the process.

<You made meat of unlife. My stomach did not feel good.>

<But I got away. I call this a win. You need to stop thinking with your stomach. Anyone can make bad meat and hurt you.>

<My stomach is very strong. Your bad meat is stronger...for now.>

It was a scary thought that at some point, he would be able to eat Healthy Hellhound Delight and suffer no dangerous side effects. Even though all the danger was suffered by anyone standing in his proximity while breathing.

If he could eat that without it negatively affecting him, he would be nearly indestructible.

Monty walked over to where we stood after gesturing and forming a strong breeze, blowing the deathane away. He created a large sausage and gave it to my semi-wary hellhound, who gave it a thorough smelling, but didn't chomp on it.

"It's a small consolation, but you deserve this after your bondmate's underhanded tactics," he said, glancing at me. "You are a good boy."

"Not underhanded, creative," I said. "Underhanded would be putting me up against a teleporting hellhound, and expecting me to avoid getting slobbered and mangled...repeatedly."

Peaches sniffed the sausage a few times more, before looking at me.

<*Is this safe?*>

<*Finally thinking before inhaling?*>

<*I don't like your bad meat. The angry man makes good meat. Did you help him make this meat?*>

<*No. It's safe. Go ahead.*>

He proceeded to scarf down the meat without a second thought.

"He can't eat everything he encounters," I continued. "He has to learn that some things aren't edible."

"It is my understanding that once he matures, your healthy meat won't have much of an effect on him," Monty said. "Mature hellhounds are terrifying creatures. Very little can stop them. It still takes a considerable number of Shadowhounds, along with several high-level mages, to stop an adult hellhound."

"Bonded or unbonded?"

"Unbonded," Monty said his voice grim as he glanced at Peaches. "A bonded adult hellhound requires a completely different strategy."

"What strategy?"

"In the case of a bonded hellhound, the human in the pair becomes the initial target," Monty said looking at me. "The hellhound in that equation is too powerful to confront directly, without removing the bondmate...first."

"So I would be the first one attacked by anyone who knew about hellhounds?"

"Attacked? No," Monty said. "They would try to *eliminate* you first. Your death *is* the method of attack. Which presents a singular dilemma for anyone encountering you two, considering your particular condition."

"Is that why I'm making people nervous?"

"Not people, entities above our current level of power," he

said as he gestured and repaired the damage to the stone caused by Peaches. "They perceive you two as a credible threat, which is not an unfounded concern. Frankly, I'm surprised an assassination contract hasn't been sanctioned."

"You're *expecting* them to come after me?" I asked, looking at my hellhound. "Us?"

"Us, yes," Monty said as he turned to leave the course. "Especially after our recent interactions with the Keepers. The moment you bonded to your creature, this was a potential outcome. Even more so, now that you're learning a battleform."

"I really need to learn that battleform."

"You both do, but *you* more than your hellhound," Monty said. "It will come naturally to him. As you grow in power so will he. I agree, I'd say a visit to Hades is in order."

"Would've been nice if hellhounds came with some kind of instruction manual," I said rubbing Peaches' oversized head. "That would've taken out some of the guesswork."

"Aside from that being patently impossible in practical terms," Monty answered, shaking his head. "I think each hellhound is unique and matures as they bond. The only one that could write such a manual for your creature is you."

I rubbed my creature's massive head as he chuffed in response and leaned into my hand, nearly making me lose my balance. He was at his core just a big ham if I overlooked who his father was, the baleful glare, teleportation, indestructible skin, oh, and the flame breath. Other than that, he was practically harmless.

"You think he will develop other abilities?"

"You mean besides noxious gastric emissions?"

"Yes, besides deathane," I said still rubbing Peaches' head. "As he gets older he seems to get new abilities. The battleform is new."

"No, it's new to you, but all hellhounds have a battleform," Monty said. "The key is learning his particular form and then surviving it."

"I wonder what Cerberus' battleform is?"

"I hope we never have to face it," Monty said and then looked away. "My uncle is on his way. That's odd, I rarely sense him on his approaches unless it's..."

A green teleportation circle formed in front of us a second later. A moment after that, Dex materialized inside the circle.

"Boys," he said his voice grim, "we have some troubling news."

FOUR

Troubling news for Dex was usually catastrophic news for anyone else. If he was concerned, the best course of action was to run in the opposite direction of whatever was coming our way.

I tried not to show any panic, took a deep breath, and let it out slowly. Monty adjusted his sleeves, removing non-existent dust as Dex approached us. He was still doing his ancient bohemian look, wearing his long hair in a loose ponytail, a white linen shirt and worn jeans. His feet were bare, but I could see thick silver toe rings on the second toe of each foot. Each ring was covered in runes and glowed a soft green.

"Toe rings?" I asked despite my concern at his announcement. "They look good."

Dex cracked a small smile, looked at his feet and wiggled his toes. Soft flickers of green light danced around his feet. I resisted the temptation to make any comments involving twinkling toes or any other kinds of toes for that matter.

"Mo made them for me," he said still wiggling his toes. "They're ley rings."

"Ley rings, as in having to do with ley-lines and that sort of thing?" I asked. I remembered our short visit to Scola Tower and how it was part of an interconnected network of ley-lines in the area. I looked around the school grounds. "You're working with ley-lines? Here?"

"Aye," he said. "They enhance my sensitivity to grounding along with other things."

"Grounding?"

"Tapping into ley-lines and nexuses of power," he said, looking around the grounds. "Especially in this place, the lines of power have to be aligned just so." He extended an arm away from us in a demonstration. "Or it will all go pear-shaped when they decide to pay us a visit."

"Who is insane enough to pay you a visit here?"

"The Elders," Monty said. "They weren't exactly pleased when my uncle decided to place the sect under new leadership."

"They stopped doing what the sect was created for," Dex said with some heat in his voice. "They grew complacent and lazy, only concerned about their power, forgetting that the teaching and creation of battlemages is, and has always been, the highest priority of the Golden Circle."

Monty nodded.

"*Si vas pacem, para bellum*," Monty said. "If you want peace, prepare for war."

"Exactly," Dex said. "They forgot that, along with many other things."

"Who? The Golden Circle Elders?" I asked. "They would dare come here uninvited?"

"Uninvited is the only way they would," Dex said with a wicked grin before growing serious again. "No. They wouldn't, not on their own at least. They would appeal to—"

"The Grand Council," Monty finished. "They've petitioned the Grand Council, haven't they?"

Dex nodded.

"It was expected," Dex said with a shrug. "They did lose an entire sect."

"Lose?" I asked. "Didn't you relocate it for them?"

"Something like that," Dex said, waving my words away. "Still, they seem to have their knickers in a twist." He looked around the grounds again. "I'd say this is a major improvement."

"Bloody hell," Monty said under his breath, shaking his head. "This is not good."

I raised a finger.

"Some of us are not educated in the details of mage life," I said. "Why is the Grand Council bad news?"

"The Grand Council oversees *all* of the sects worldwide," Monty explained. "If they move against us, they have vast resources at their disposal to make our lives…difficult."

"And shorter," Dex said. "They rarely act against individuals, but when they do, it's usually to eliminate what they consider a problem."

"Or a potential problem," Monty added. "The Grand Council believes in the policy of eliminating the problem before it becomes one. If a tree branch contains rot, the Grand Council overcorrects by removing the entire tree, roots and all. It's an archaic, heavy-handed institution that lacks any semblance of tact or nuance."

"They default to scorched earth maneuvers?"

"On a good day," Monty answered. "They are slow to act, but once in motion—"

"Difficult to stop, like most large bureaucracies," Dex finished. "They are large enough to have depth and breadth, and complex enough to possess plausible deniability. Most of the time, one branch of the Grand Council doesn't know what the others are doing."

"Then we should be okay, right?" I asked. "I mean, why

would *we* get their attention? They're dealing with things on a worldwide scale—big picture kind of stuff. Why would they be interested in us?"

"Normally, we wouldn't get their attention," Monty said turning to Dex. "My uncle on the other hand…"

"It's very likely some of the Golden Circle Elders voiced their disapproval at my relocation of the sect," Dex said. "Something like that won't go unanswered. It presents an existential threat."

"There aren't many mages who could accomplish what you did," Monty said. "Completely relocating an entire sect is a grave issue because of the scope of the act."

"When you say it won't go unanswered," I said. "What exactly does that mean? Will they send you a strongly written letter or some other kind of message?"

Dex smiled and chilled my blood.

"Not exactly," he said. "They tend to be a bit more vigorous in their responses."

"Why does vigorous sound like violent in this context?"

"Because it is," Monty said. "Have they contacted you, uncle?"

"You two need to get back," Dex said, brushing Monty's question aside. "If they decide to visit, which I find unlikely unless an Emissary is involved—"

"An Emissary?" Monty said, turning suddenly to face Dex. "They wouldn't send an Emissary unless—"

"I may have strongly disregarded some of their earlier messages to return the Golden Circle," Dex said. "I've been busy."

"At what point do they send an Emissary?" I asked, even more confused. "Because that sounds like one of those last-resort moves."

"Emissaries are the enforcement arm of the Grand Council," Monty explained. "If my uncle disregarded previous attempts at communication, they will treat him as a rogue mage who is actively hostile toward the Grand Council...an enemy of the Council."

"Which is why you need to get back," Dex said. "I've made several provisions for your safety. Proximity to me is not safe right now."

"Provisions for our safety?" I asked as Dex formed a large teleportation circle under us. "Why would you need to make provisions for *our* safety?"

"Weren't you paying attention?" Dex asked as he gestured. "The Grand Council deals with problems by eliminating everything they think is connected to the problem."

I nodded.

"I got that," I said. "They rip out the tree by the roots for a rotting branch."

"Exactly," he said. "Tree and roots are connected. If they can't act directly against me, they will act against those connected to me, my family."

"What about Peanut and Cece?" I asked concerned for the young girls. "Are they in danger?"

"They are in an undisclosed location and being personally protected by Mo," Dex said. "They are not in the slightest amount of danger—unlike you three."

"They wouldn't attack us, would they?" I asked with a chuckle, waving his words away. My chuckle died a short-lived life when neither Monty nor Dex joined me. "They would?"

"They've done worse for less," Dex said. "If you're found here, they will execute a kill order on all three of you for aiding and abetting in my relocation of the Golden Circle sect. No further reason would be needed."

"Relocation...you mean stealing?"

"Semantics," he said. "If they visit you at your home, the

worst they can do is warn you to stay away from me. If they find you here, they can and will dispatch Sanitizers."

"Sanitizers," I said. "No explanation needed. Different name, but I'm guessing the same job description—assassin mages?"

"Some of the best, or worst, depending on where you're standing when they unleash their casts," he said. "But that's putting the cart before the horse. You three should be fine, as long as you're not here when they visit."

"They're coming aren't they?" Monty asked. "You're delaying them somehow?"

"Something along those lines," Dex said, gazing off to the side. "I've rearranged the entrance passage to make it...interesting. They won't all make it through, but those who do will require I pay them some attention."

"You're going to attack Grand Council members?" Monty asked in disbelief. "That could start a war."

"Do you really think members of the Grand Council will come here?" Dex asked, his voice filled with a quiet menace. "I know them. Not one would be willing to face me. No, they will send lackeys and proxies. They will use words and when those fail, they will use force."

"What will you do?" I asked. "That sounds bad."

"I will let them speak," Dex said. "Then I will send them back—alive."

"And then?" Monty asked. "You're not one to leave something like that alone. What will you do after you send back the messengers?"

"Then I will go have a conversation with the Grand Council," he said. "I'm sure we can agree on a solution that doesn't involve spilling blood."

Monty looked grim but nodded.

I had a feeling that the Grand Council had no idea what it was doing messing with Dex, and if they did, they were basically tired of living and looking for a violent way out of this life.

Dex gave Peaches a pat on the head and rubbed behind his ears, before producing a large sausage and giving it to my hellhound, who proceeded to hoover it into his belly.

"But you said you took precautions," I said, admiring the velocity of my hellhound's suction capability. "If you think we'll be fine, why are you taking precautions?"

"Better to be a warrior in a garden *and* a gardener capable of war," Dex said, mangling several sayings at once. "I'm not old by accident, boy. I'm old because I anticipated what my enemies were willing to do, then I went beyond their willingness. Remember that."

"Remember?" I said confused. "I'm barely understanding what you're trying to say."

"Understood," Monty said. "We'll keep a low profile for as long as possible."

"If things do get interesting," Dex said. "The Boutique and others have been notified. There is a contingency plan in place in case the Grand Council is being duplicitous."

"A contingency plan?" I asked. "One of those, 'break glass in case of massive attack by lying mages' kind of contingency plans?"

"Very close, but this is more along the lines of 'unleash our own scary mages' kind of plan. Let's hope it doesn't come to that, but it's the Grand Council. Subtlety and tact have never been their strong suits. They tend to lean toward deceit and subterfuge."

"You can't tell us this plan?" Monty asked. "We would be better prepared if they did attack."

"No," Dex said, his voice serious. "If they do act as expected, your initial response must be authentic. Also, they must think you're vulnerable. It will shape how they approach you."

Monty nodded.

"The Boutique?" I asked. "What do you mean, the Boutique?"

"Time to go," Dex said with a nod. "I'll visit when I can."

Dex gestured and the school disappeared in a green flash.

FIVE

We arrived at the Moscow a few seconds later.

My body arrived at one moment and the rest of my digestive system arrived a few seconds later. The wave of nausea hit me like an uppercut and I took a few moments to orient myself.

Even Monty looked off from the sudden teleport. The only one who looked unaffected was Peaches, which wasn't surprising.

"That was peculiar," Monty said, steadying himself against a wall. "My uncle's teleports usually have no side-effects. He must be extremely concerned. Did you suffer any ill effects?"

"Ill-effects? I don't know what you mean," I lied. "Maybe you're not used to teleports like some of us?"

"I'm also not turning green like some of you, either," he said. "How bad was it?"

"The usual, nausea and my stomach catching up to my body a few seconds later," I said with a groan. "I thought I was over that."

"You mostly are," Monty said. "This was an unusual rapid

teleport cast with little to no prep. The temporal effects are more pronounced when that kind of teleport is executed."

"I'm glad he doesn't do that more often," I said, grabbing my stomach. "My body wouldn't be able to take it."

"Nor mine," he said, heading to the kitchen. "I need a strong cuppa."

I followed him into the kitchen and prepared myself a large mug of Death Wish, complete with my javambrosia. While that was in the works, I filled my hellhound's titanium bowl with prime pastrami from Ezra's to fill that black hole he called a stomach.

Part of that was to keep him well fed. He *was* growing and eating more and more these days. The other part was an apology for my broccoli-laced meat attack in the obstacle-labyrinth.

<*I'm sorry about the healthy meat, boy. To be fair, you were trying to slobber-mangle me.*>

<*The angry man promised me extra meat if I found you fast and stopped you. Extra meat is good. You are my bondmate, I would never hurt you. My saliva heals.*>

<*I know, which is why I'm filling your bowl with meat from the place. Enjoy. Meat is life.*>

He proceeded to inhale the meat in the bowl. I was seriously going to have to consider a bigger bowl and a larger space for hellhound romping. He was getting huge.

Once my Death Wish was ready, I took a moment to inhale the thick, rich aroma of coffee goodness, before the first sip jolted my brain into full-blown functionality.

With a sigh of pleasure, I felt my brain and the world return to some sense of normalcy. It wasn't full-blown, because my world will never be what I used to consider normal ever again, but with my coffee, it came close.

Monty stared at me for a few seconds before focusing on his tea.

"Do you ever understand what he's trying to say when he gets all wise like that and mangles several sayings at once?" I asked, between sips of coffee as Monty walked around our space, reinforcing our defenses. "I didn't understand half of what he said."

Monty gestured and sent symbols in every direction. Near the entrance and at every hallway junction, I saw him activate dark red circles.

They looked angry and dangerous.

"Are those—?"

"Obliteration circles, yes," he said, touching the outer symbols around the circles. "They are keyed to us, which means we can traverse them and suffer no harm. The outcome will be devastating to anyone who tries to invade this space."

"Even Peaches?"

"Yes, your creature, which is nigh indestructible, won't be affected by these circles," he said. "I can't say the same for anyone else. As to my uncle, it's best to look for the message behind the words."

"That's easy to do when you understand the words," I answered after taking another sip. "The thing is, it sometimes feels like Dex is on another plane of conversation when he's talking. It's like he has several conversations happening all at once, except I can barely understand the one I'm involved in. He talks in a way that's beyond mage-speak. Dex-speak makes mage-speak feel clear and that's saying something since mages hardly ever make sense."

"True," Monty said, placing his hands on certain parts of our main door, which was currently rune-inscribed titanium. His actions caused sections of the door to glow a bright orange before growing dim again. "The meaning of his words are usually embedded in the words behind the words—the unspoken things he's not saying."

"The shadow conversation," I said with a sudden insight. "I have to listen for the conversation that can't be heard?"

"Crude, but yes," Monty said with a nod. "The words behind the words."

"Should I also listen for the one hand clapping and the sound of the tree that falls in the empty forest?" I asked. "How about the sensation of the breeze on the still wind, or what was my original face before I was born?"

"Very good questions," Monty said still focused on the defenses. "You forgot to ask, what is the color of the wind?"

"Don't even start," I said, glaring at him. "I haven't had all of my coffee."

"The fact that you can bring up those examples means you are beginning to grasp the words behind the words."

I shook my head in disbelief.

"The words behind the words," I repeated softly. "That's exactly what I mean. Dex speaks like that all the time, most mages do, although you've gotten better over time."

"I haven't changed, your understanding has increased," he said. "My manner of speech has remained the same, but you have encountered beings and situations that have forced you to grow and expand your understanding, revealing the meaning of things to you with more ease—though my uncle is a special case. Even I find him challenging to comprehend at times."

"That means there's no hope for me getting his meaning," I said, watching him activate the door. "What exactly are you doing? You really think something is going to get through *that* door?"

He stopped for a moment to examine the door.

"No defense is fully impenetrable," he said. "The runes on this door are formidable, as are the defenses in our space. They can withstand a frontal assault, yes, but not indefinitely. Even this door can be breached."

"Well, now I feel extra secure," I said, shaking my head. "If it can't hold off an assault, what are you doing, then?"

"I'm making sure our defenses are in place," he said. "We have to get ready. The door would be our third line of defense. Actually the space around our front door outside would be the second line of defense, right after the perimeter runes around the Moscow activated which is our first line of defense."

"Anyone ever accuse you of being paranoid?" I asked. "Does Olga know of all the 'extra' defenses you've placed around her building?"

"No," he said. "I see no need to inform her. Most, if not all the defenses are passive and designed to keep the inhabitants of the Moscow safe. There's no need to worry her needlessly about failsafes and defenses."

"Also, you don't want to face an angry, ice-queen Olga, if she doesn't like your idea of defenses," I said with a smile before taking another sip of my coffee. "I'm surprised she doesn't have defenses of her own."

"She does," Monty said. "Most of the defenses I have in place enhance the ones she set up. Either increasing the intensity or lethality where appropriate. The new defenses I've learned recently will help us get ready."

His words filled me with a mild amount of dread.

It wasn't fear, but the fact that Dex had taken precautions meant something was headed our way. Something major. I had no problem with that—well actually I did, but what concerned me more was the uncertainty.

Who or what exactly was coming our way?

SIX

"Dex said we really shouldn't worry too much about it. What I'm seeing you do is the opposite of that. He said we should be fine. Why are you 'getting ready'? Getting ready for what exactly?"

He turned from the door to glance at me.

"How strong would you say my uncle is, as a mage?"

The question threw me for a second.

"What?" I asked and gave it some thought. "I don't know. He's stronger than most or all mages I know. Even the Ten, who are in a league of badassery of their own, show him a healthy respect. Gods seem to treat him as a mage to be wary of and don't go out of their way to get on his bad side. That means he's a heavy hitter."

"Where would you place him in terms of strength?"

"If I had to guess, I would say just this side of Supreme Ultra Archmage," I said. "Strong enough to make gods rethink their life choices by going against him."

"That's not an actual classification," Monty said. "Anywhere."

"It should be. Well there's the whole Harbinger thing," I said. "With that title, I wouldn't even dare guess his power level. He foreshadows Death with a capital D. That has to be off-the-charts power."

"I would say that's a fair, if not entirely accurate, gauge of his power," Monty said after a moment of thought. "Now, consider that my uncle, in light of what he anticipates is a future conflict, has taken precautions against what he perceives we will face. What does that tell you?"

I gave it some thought.

If Dex was taking precautions, it was probably a good idea to start looking for some off-plane living. Some place where we could be safe until his conflict with the Grand Council blew over.

"It tells me that this would be a good time to visit Orethe's Underworld château for a century or two, or at least until Dex finishes his *conversations* with the Grand Council?"

"Not a possibility at the moment, I'm afraid," he said. "We can't be seen running or hiding. It would send the wrong message."

"The wrong message to who?" I asked. "Who would get this wrong message?"

"Whom. To those who are watching us," Monty said. "Make no mistake, we *are* being watched and it's not Orethe's Underworld château—it's yours."

"So a prolonged hiatus to Ore—my Underworld château is not an option?"

"No, not at the moment," he answered. "I also think Hades would have some words on the matter. While the home is yours, it resides in the Underworld—a plane under his direct control."

"I'm not exactly comfortable with that idea."

"I didn't think you would be."

"Still, I distinctly remember the whole 'you should be fine' part of Dex's conversation," I said. "Why would he say that if he didn't mean it?"

"He did mean it, but he also said he took *precautions*," Monty said reinforcing the casts around the door. "When *my* uncle takes precautions, it's time to make sure *all* the defenses are in place. Again, you have to listen for the message in the words. If I were you, I'd make sure I had enough ammunition for your gun."

"Persuader rounds?"

"If the Grand Council comes after us, persuading them of anything is off the table," he said. "Sanitizers don't negotiate or take prisoners, and Emissaries are devoutly loyal to the Grand Council, willing to sacrifice their lives for the cause."

"Everything except persuaders then," I said, moving to our ammo room located off the reception area, but before the conference room. "How dangerous exactly is the Grand Council?"

"To us? Normally I would say the danger is negligible," he said, materializing his blades, the Sorrows. "We are so far below their radar that we shouldn't register as a threat."

"Somehow, I'm getting the feeling that's not the case for Dex," I said. "How did he piss them off?"

"My uncle possesses the uncanny ability to anger some of the most dangerous beings in existence," Monty said. "Though I suspect it's not entirely anger directed toward him."

"It's not anger, it's fear," I said. "Dex scares most of them because they can't control him or match his cunning. When faced with someone like Dex, they are operating with the unknown and the unknown creates fear. I know firsthand he can be scary, especially when he pulls out that weapon of his."

Monty nodded.

"Nemain can be quite fearsome, agreed," Monty replied. "He rarely uses it any more, those days are mostly behind him."

"I would say that fear is the driving factor. That, and the whole 'you won't mind if I just borrow this sect' move he pulled on the Golden Circle."

"This goes beyond his appropriation of the Golden Circle sect, though I'm certain that plays a huge part," Monty said, producing a special cloth and gently rubbing the blades of the Sorrows. "He literally relocated—"

"Stole," I interrupted. "He *stole* an entire sect. Let's call it what it is. He didn't think *that* would create some kind of response? How many mages can even do that?"

"Not many," Monty admitted. "It requires a higher level of skill in teleportation and vast power. My uncle possesses both in excess."

"Not many?" I asked. "There are mages as strong as Dex?"

"As strong or stronger," Monty answered. "Yes. They just don't go around relocating entire sects."

"He had to expect some reaction," I said. "You can't just take a sect, I mean, okay, he did, but that's going to get a reaction from whoever is the head of the sects, the Grand Council in this case."

Monty nodded.

"My uncle is quite savvy," Monty said, still focused on the blades. "I'm certain he knew there would be some kind of backlash, and honestly, knowing him, he precipitated this confrontation intentionally."

"Why would he do that?" I asked. "Why would he deliberately piss off the Grand Council?"

"There's some history there, history that's not mine to share," Monty said, putting the cloth away and examining the symbols on the Sorrows. "Suffice to say, there are no

Montagues on the Grand Council and that's due mostly to my uncle. The animosity that exists there predates my life and that of many Montagues. I don't even know all of the details. What I do know for sure is that my uncle was invited to sit on the Grand Council at its inception."

"Let me guess, he politely declined?"

"Not so politely," Monty replied, still examining his blades. "He told them he would never join a mutual appreciation society."

"That doesn't sound so bad," I said. "In fact that almost sounds tactful and very un-Dex-like."

"He also added that they should take their invitation and stuff it with extreme violence, wishing them a painful death as they did so."

"Ouch," I said, shaking my head. "Okay, that sounds more like Dex. Groups like that don't tolerate slights or insults well. They have long memories and hold angry, lethal grudges."

"And they are patient," Monty said, absorbing his blades. "They are willing to wait for what they feel is a legitimate excuse to act against their enemies, perceived or real."

"An excuse like taking over an entire sect and oh, I don't know, moving it off-plane?"

"That would be a perfect reason for them to act," Monty said. "And yet they didn't, at least not initially. No, something else has set them off."

"Do they really have a reason to go after Dex, besides borrowing the Golden Circle, and his blowing them off with insults to their delicate egos?"

"Yes, insubordination, usurping of an established sect, a definitive and prolonged indication of rogue activity, associating with a clandestine group of incredibly powerful mages with no known sect affiliation, destroying norms that have been established for centuries, and engaging in establishing a school of active warfare. Any *one* of those charges is enough to declare an erasure on the offending mage."

"Active warfare?" I asked. "How is he engaging in active warfare?"

"A school of battlemagic advances the necessity of battlemages," he said. "Battlemages are mages, yes, but they have a very specific and narrow focus."

"Battle."

"Not battle, war," Monty answered, his tone dark. "Battlemages are created and trained to fight in wars. The magical community at large has deemed battlemages obsolete and unnecessary."

"You can't say that for certain," I said, giving him a doubtful look. "How can you say that? We've faced plenty of mages who knew how to fight."

"The Golden Circle was once one of the largest sects in the entire magical community," Monty said. "It was required for all mages, no matter the discipline, to spend no less than twenty years training at the Golden Circle."

"To learn how to fight?"

"In the case of another Supernatural War, we would not be caught off-guard," Monty said. "Training at the Golden Circle enhanced what skills you possessed or taught you new ones you could use to defend yourself and others. Over time, that changed."

"Let me guess. No wars," I said.

Monty nodded.

"So why do we need a school of battlemagic?"

"The Elders at the Golden Circle became lax," Monty said. "They allowed the curriculum to be modified. Certain teachings, which were once mandatory were altered or removed altogether."

"They were creating paper tigers," I said. "Battlemages in name only."

"Worse. Even the term battlemage, which was once a title bestowed with respect, became seen as derogatory," Monty said. "They stripped it of its history, of all honor, and made it something to be reviled. It used to be the driving purpose of the Golden Circle."

"If I didn't know better, I'd say this was some long-term plan to weaken the magical community," I said, pulling out boxes of ammo. "Take out the soldiers and those who teach them, and all you're left with are the people who can't fight. Easy targets, easy to manipulate and control."

"My uncle felt the same way, which is why he did what he did."

"Still seems a bit extreme," I said. "Why not ask the Golden Circle to reinstate the battlemage curriculum?"

"He did, several times," Monty said. "His request was rejected every time. The official response was: 'Refused Without Consideration.'"

"That sounds short-sighted," I said. "If there is one thing I've learned from stepping into your world, it's that there are always battles that need fighting."

"It would seem we are on the precipice of another," Monty said. "This one will have far-reaching consequences. There is a chance of a civil war in the magical community if this is handled poorly."

"Which is why we can't sit this one out?" I asked. "We may need to run interference? Can I just remind you that our tact track record is nothing to brag about?"

"Be that as it may, we may be one of the few factors in preventing another large-scale magical war," he said. "We must remain on this plane and prevent this from escalating further."

"What is the clandestine group of incredibly powerful mages with no known sect affiliation that Dex is connected to?" I asked. "As far as I know, he doesn't belong to any group, with good reason. What group could he possibly belong to? The Apocalypse Mages? When the end is near, we'll protect your rear?"

"As usual, your humor fails to entertain," he said. "Though in this case, you are not too far off."

"He belongs to the Apocalypse Mages?" I asked incredulous. "That's a real group?"

He stared at me for a good five seconds.

"Don't be silly, there is no group with that name. However, he does belong to a clandestine mage group with no known affiliation."

"No way," I said. "I always thought with Mo as his partner and his past as Harbinger, no group would be insane enough to ask him to be a member. I find it hard to believe."

"Agreed, but it's true. It's not common knowledge, and no one will actually admit it," Monty said. "Dex is a full member of the Ten. His unofficial role is very official when it comes to matters of import. I wouldn't be surprised if he was one of the founders of the group."

"What?" I said somewhat stunned. "He's never admitted to being part of the Ten. Actually, it's been the opposite. He actively denies it."

"And he never will admit it," Monty said. "Nor will any of the members of the Ten, unless the situation calls for a formal recognition of his status within the group."

"Then how do *you* know?"

"Research. Professor Ziller primarily, along with some other unorthodox methods I'm not at liberty to divulge at the moment," he said. "I've learned that every member of the Ten carries one specific rune on their body."

"What kind of rune?" I asked. "Why would they need a special rune?"

"It is given to members of the Ten to call out to each other in times of need."

"In times of need?" I said. "I would imagine that doesn't happen often."

"No, not often at all," Monty said. "Can you imagine a situation where a member of the Ten would need to call for help?"

"Sure, end-of-the-world, apocalypse-type scenarios come to mind," I said, as I thought about it. "Each of the Ten are scary in their own right. The world better be ending if they have to face a threat as a group."

"True. In any case," Monty continued, "the vetting process to get this rune is beyond torturous. From my research, to survive the initiation phase alone requires the candidate mage to be at or near Archmage level."

"Dex is beyond that—easily," I said. "But that doesn't mean he's part of the Ten."

"Agreed, however, there is one qualifier that sets each member of the Ten apart from other mages," Monty said. "One that has ostracized them from their respective sects."

"I thought it was their power levels? They were too strong to be in their sects and were kicked out."

"That is the accepted cover story. The truth is darker, much darker," Monty said. "Each member of the Ten has served Death—capital D as you like to say, in some way, and more importantly...survived their time of service."

"I'd say being the Harbinger of Death qualifies." I didn't see all of the pieces fall into place. Enough of them did, so that it made sense, but I had the feeling I was missing the bigger picture. "Have you seen this special rune?"

"No," he said. "I'm still working on it."

My stunned brain seized for a moment.

"You're still *working* on it?" I asked surprised. "Why are

you even working on it? What made you pursue this in the first place?"

"Much of my uncle is a mystery...even to me," he said. "There are things I want—need to know."

"Why not ask him?"

"As open and transparent as my uncle is, he is also astoundingly reticent to discuss personal matters, despite the fact that I am his family," he said. "Do you know that I didn't learn about his plan for the Montague School of Battlemagic until after the fact?"

"Dex doesn't come across as the type to ask permission," I said. "He does what he does and everyone around him adjusts, or they don't. I don't think he cares too much about what other people think—family included."

"That is and has always been evident," Monty said, somewhat upset. "But something like this? He should have informed me."

"I disagree. I think you need to factor in that there are things he knows that you shouldn't know," I said. "One of those, 'it's safer if you don't know' kind of situations. The school feels that way."

"That I can understand. There were plenty of need-to-know situations during the war," he said. "But we are in a different kind of conflict now. Operational obfuscation can cost us dearly. Transparency is the best course of action."

"Right, which is why instead of asking *him* about all this, you're doing your investigation *without* telling him," I said. "Sounds extra transparent."

"I *have* asked him and he has refused to answer beyond certain points in my inquiry," he said. "Told me to stop Sherlocking his life. That I would not enjoy some of the things I discovered."

I couldn't help smiling at Dex's response, turning a name into a verb.

"That sounds like great advice," I said. "You should listen and even better, you should follow it. Do you really want to know everything about him? Really?"

"Yes, *really*."

"Why?" I asked, curious. "It sounds like a recipe for disaster. I'm sure the skeletons he has in his closet should never, ever see the light of day."

"To face what's coming, we need power," he said. "One of the ways to acquire that power, which doesn't include blood or dark magic, resides with the Ten. If he's one of the Ten, then he—"

I shook my head and laughed.

"That almost sounds like you want to join the Ten."

Monty remained serious, stared and shook his head.

"It's one of the limited ways to acquire power without going dark or engaging in forbidden rituals with blood magic," he said. "I do think it would be prudent to join the Ten. As a solution, it's ideal. Both of us should be part of the Ten."

"What do you mean *us*?" I said. "You said it yourself, to join the Ten you have to have insane amounts of power, at or near Archmage level. That may include *you* after all the recent Keeper business, but that definitely does *not* include me."

"You are viewing the definition of power too narrowly."

"No, I don't think so," I said, shaking my head slowly. "My view is pretty broad. I know for a fact, I am nowhere near LD's or TK's level of power. That's not an educated guess, that's an educated fact. Besides, what makes you think they would even consider the idea? We don't exactly run in their circles. They are rogue mages."

"We don't exactly conform to the norms ourselves," he said. "We could easily be classified as rogue."

"You use that word, but I don't think it means what you think it means," I said. "They take rogue to new depths of devastation. We are awesome at property damage and pissing off some powerful mages. They deal with things way above our pay grade."

"I'm sure you've noticed our enemies have gotten stronger."

"Monty, this is beyond punching above our weight class, this is asking to get painfully squished," I said. "I don't think we are ready to step into their world."

"I don't think we will be given a choice," Monty said. "Dex informed the Boutique, which means he prepped the Ten, or at the very least LD and TK."

"I did catch that," I said. "It means that whatever he's about to face with the Grand Council is serious. That doesn't mean we can become honorary members of the Ten."

"Nothing ventured, nothing gained," he said. "When I next see them, I will ask for acceptance into the Ten...for the both of us."

"What makes you think they would even consider your request?" I asked. "I mean besides the fact that we are not in their league."

"You underestimate yourself," he said. "I have worn the mantle of Harbinger and wielded Nemain, I'll admit it was brief, but I was able to survive the experience."

"Survive the experience?" I asked. "Excuse me? What's that supposed to mean?"

"Wearing the mantle of Harbinger has been known to hasten the demise of the person wearing it, if they are unprepared or incompatible," he said matter-of-factly. I stared at him in stunned silence. "If I was an improper match, I would not have survived the experience. Not for long at least."

"And you're just telling me this now, Mr. Transparency? Dex let you do this knowing it could have killed you?"

"You do have a point, my apologies for not sharing that information earlier," he said. "As for you, you have a unique *understanding* with Badb Catha and you happen to be the Marked of Kali. I'd say both those situations make you eminently qualified for consideration into the Ten."

"I disagree. Wait a second," I said, hearing Peaches rumble as the energy pressure around us increased. I reached for Grim Whisper as I saw Monty gesture. "That feels—"

We were both too slow as the windows to our space imploded.

SEVEN

I never managed to finish my sentence.

A blast of thunder filled our space, drowning out everything, including my thoughts. The force of the wave knocked Monty and me back. My hellhound hunkered down against the blast, but remained where he stood.

The sound was overwhelming.

I wouldn't have been surprised if a freight train had crashed into the Moscow, deciding that the best route through the building was through our reception area.

At once, all the windows were shattered. The building rocked and swayed slightly as the glass shards sliced through the living room in an effort to shred us to pieces.

Despite his size and weight, I managed to grab Peaches and pull him behind a counter in the kitchen as sharp glass shards sliced the air past us.

In a fraction of a second, part of my brain registered the broken windows and clinically noted that the barrage of glass was going to cause major damage and pain.

Another part of my brain, the one that still held on to things like ideas about what is possible and impossible, and struggled daily with being thrust into this world of magic, told me that the swarm of glass headed our way should have been impossible.

All of the glass, every single window in our space, was runed to prevent this kind of destruction. At least that's what I was told. It seemed that Monty didn't count on this much force slamming into the windows at once.

He had taken precautions.

We had enemies and he knew that the windows would be easy to use as weapons in a scenario very similar to the one we were facing right now.

Monty jumped into action and finished his gesture, throwing up a shield as I abandoned going for my gun and materialized my dawnward.

The glass, surprised me by slicing through parts of Monty's shield, narrowly avoiding us. Another large shard punctured a section of my dawnward, burying itself into one of the kitchen cabinets.

Whoever launched this attack had done their homework.

"The runed glass can cut through the shields," I said behind a counter with Peaches next to me. Monty slid in next to me a moment later. "How did they shatter the glass? It was runed. Wasn't it runed? I thought everything was supposed to stop once it hit the dawnward or your shield."

"There are limits and tolerances," Monty said raising an eyebrow at the pieces of glass buried in the wall opposite us. "It would seem this attack exceeds the tolerances of our defenses."

"You think?" I asked, looking at the shattered windows. "We nearly got shish kebabbed by all this glass. How did it get past your shield? I get it cutting through my dawnward, but your shield should have stopped the glass."

"These are not glass skewers; the correct terminology would most likely be shredded by the glass, not shish kebabbed," he said. "As for *how* the glass managed to puncture my shield, I would say this is no low-level mage attack. To shatter that runed glass would take considerable power."

"I thought it was runically enhanced to be shatterproof?" I asked concerned. "Didn't you say it was shatterproof?"

"Runically enhanced, yes," Monty said, brushing off some of the smaller pieces of glass from his sleeves. "I believe my words were *shatter-resistant* to be precise. That means it's shatter-proof to a limited degree."

"Olga is going to have a massive fit at all this damage," I said, realizing that most of our floors were covered in glass now. "You know how she gets with damage to the Moscow."

"I think we have greater concerns at the moment than our irate landlady," Monty said, closing his eyes. "There's a surge near the door."

"A surge near the door? A surge of what?"

He turned suddenly to the door.

"The opening attack is a distraction," he continued, lifting me to my feet as he created a shield, reinforced by a golden lattice of energy. "The real attack is coming from—"

I saw the door flare orange in several sections.

"Conference room!" I yelled as we ran to the other end of our space. Peaches blinked out and got there before us, hunkering down under the table with a low rumble followed by a dangerous growl. "Good, boy. Stay away from the door until we know what's going on."

"The door is going to—" Monty started.

The door wasn't Australian Buloke.

In hindsight, we probably should've replaced the door long ago with reinforced Australian Buloke. Considering the quality of our recent enemies, leaving the door as is could easily qualify as a security oversight.

Especially when whoever was out there had just cut

through our windows as if they were plain glass. I gazed out again at our current door, which was runed titanium.

I realized that as strong as it was, it was no match for whatever cast broke through our window defenses, which meant the conference room doors would last all of half a second. We made it to the conference room as Monty slammed the doors closed behind us.

"Monty you need to reinforce the doors," I said, keeping my eyes on the front door, which I could easily see from where I stood. "If that cast can tear past the windows and get through the front door, these doors are going to be as strong as wet tissue paper."

"Unless I reinforce the runes in the wood," he said, tracing some symbols into the doors. The conference room doors gave off a deep orange glow which didn't exactly fill me with confidence when I saw the very robust titanium door begin to buckle under the force of the cast that was punching into it from the other side. "That should mitigate some of the incoming damage."

"Some?" I asked concerned. "How much is some?"

"Most," Monty said. "Which is less than all, but more than none."

The sound of tearing metal drowned out all the other noise in the next second as the front door tore off its hinges, becoming a guided door missile of destruction headed our way at speed.

"Monty, would a dawnward even make sense?"

"No," he said creating another golden lattice, which merged with the conference room doors. "The front door is more heavily runed than the windows. Your dawnward would do nothing to stop it."

"But your lattice will?"

"Alone, no," he said still focused on the door heading our

way. "But with the conference room doors in front of us, we have a better chance. I think they will hold."

As soon as he finished his sentence, the titanium door rammed into the conference room doors. The front door wasn't completely intact. The force of whatever ripped it off its hinges had torn away pieces of it, which was probably the only reason why the smaller doors were still in one piece.

The debris from the front door crashed into the conference room doors, causing damage, but not breaking through. When the dust had settled somewhat, I noticed movement in the hallway outside the front door. A figure stood there, the image becoming clearer, although the dust from the blast hid some of the features of our violent uninvited guest.

It took a few seconds but after a while, I could see the man more clearly. I didn't recognize him but that didn't mean anything. Monty had enough enemies for the both of us. My status as Marked of Kali hadn't made me any friends either. For all I knew, this could've easily been some new and improved successor Kali had sent my way.

Judging from his expression, which was a cross between angry and repulsed, my first guess was this was a pissed-off mage who didn't want to actually come inside our space because we were contagious or had some disease—like poor taste.

He wore the typical mageiform, black suit, off-white shirt, and a deep gold-colored tie. Even from where I stood, I could tell he was wearing a very high-end runed Armani bespoke ensemble.

Something about him nagged at my memory.

His suit was sharp and worthy of an established mage. It wasn't quite Monty's Zegna mage look, but it *was* impressive considering that whoever was standing at our front door, had literally blown out the windows and the door off our home.

There was, however, something familiar—the tie. I had seen a tie like that in the past, I just couldn't place it.

"The tie, Monty," I said under my breath. "Where have I seen a tie like that? I feel like I should know that tie for some reason."

Then it came back to me in a rush.

"It should," Monty said. "The first Goat was disintegrated by someone wearing a similar tie. I can only assume the man at our entrance is—"

"A magistrate," I finished, saying the title like a curse. "He dressed the same way as the one who melted the Goat."

The man at the door raised an eyebrow and nodded in our direction with a small smile as he leaned in slightly and swept the interior of our home with his gaze.

A strong vibe of disappointment made its way over to where I stood. The arrogance was strong in this one.

"This is your domicile, your home, oui?" the man asked with a sniff as he looked around again. "How...positively quaint and common."

His voice had a pronounced accent, which reminded me of Claude and...Julien. None of the memories that rushed back were pleasant ones.

"It was until you exploded the hell out of the windows and door," I said, giving him the once-over. "Now it looks like a warzone, thank you very much. I'm going to guess from the accent that you are not Dark Council."

"Dark Council," he scoffed, saying the words like they left a bad taste in his mouth. "No, I am not from the...Dark Council."

"Didn't think so, your ego is several sizes too large to fit through the doorway, unless you plan on blowing out the entrance even more to accommodate it," I said giving him a glare and a smile that clearly spelled out several choice insults. "Who are you, then?"

"I am Magistrate Emeric," the man said with an accent that screamed French and entitled from the doorway. "Direct Assistant to Emissary Alain Dubois of the Grand Council."

"Dubois?" Monty said under his breath. "Bloody hell, of course, it's Dubois."

"Ah, you know the Emissary?" Emeric asked with a pleased smile that wasn't entirely friendly. "This is to be expected. He is well known within and without the Grand Council."

"Only by reputation," Monty said. "He goes by a different name in less illustrious circles."

Emeric's expression darkened.

"Less illustrious circles?" the magistrate asked. "What is this name?"

"Perhaps you've heard of it?" Monty asked innocently. "Most mages, who are not seeking to curry favor with the Emissary or the Grand Council, call him the Bloody Scythe."

EIGHT

"The Bloody Scythe?" Emeric said with a smile that masked the pain he wanted to inflict on Monty for insulting his Emissary. "The Bloody Scythe?"

"I see you *have* heard of it," Monty said with a slight nod at the magistrate who was slowly turning a nice shade of red as he tried to hide his anger. "That's good. Do you know why he is referred this way?"

"I'm going to guess it's not his cheerful personality?" I said. "How *did* he earn such a name?"

Judging from the look on Emeric's face, he *had* heard of the name and he didn't like it one bit. For the slightest moment, a brief slip, I saw the magistrate's self-assured demeanor drop into something darker and uglier.

He quickly recovered, hiding his real expression.

He may have been acting civil and polite, but beneath that facade was a man with power who enjoyed inflicting pain on those who held less power.

This was the kid you would catch ripping the wings off flies and then watching to see what would happen. It was the same individual who poured boiling water into an ant colony to watch the ants, those who survived the initial boiling, fleeing the anthill.

People like him only became worse once they had access to power. They usually grew up into psychopaths or, like in this case, assistants to Emissaries who wielded their power unchecked.

"This...is *not* his name, this...is an insult," Emeric corrected, his voice tight. "The Emissary's correct name, is Emissary Alain Dubois and you will address him in this way at all times. And you will refer to me as Magistrate Emeric."

"Emreek?" I asked and glanced at Monty. "Is he saying he reeks? If that's the case, he should stay way over there. I've already dealt with hellhound deathane today. My nose can't handle more toxic fumes."

I tried to sense his energy signature and drew a blank, which was impossible. That meant one of two things, either he didn't have enough energy to register for a significant signature, or judging from the shattered runed glass all over the floor and mangled titanium that used to be our front door, he was much stronger than he was letting on.

I was leaning toward the second.

"It's his *name*," Monty said under his breath. "Don't make any sudden movements and don't antagonize him. He is more dangerous than he appears. His energy signature is masked under several layers of cloaking."

"I kind of figured, seeing as how he's a blank, but still able to blow up our home," I said keeping my voice low. "Have you pissed off any magistrates lately?"

"None that I'm aware of, but there's always the possibility."

Emeric cleared his throat getting our attention, again.

"This is the residence of Tristan Montague and Simon Strong, oui?" Emeric asked. "The Montague and Strong Detective Agency?"

I glared at him again, a clear three on the glare-o-meter. I considered pushing it to four, but then I'd have to draw Grim Whisper to deliver it properly, which could start all kinds of physical conversations. I opted for keeping it verbal…for now.

"You mean you weren't *sure*?" I yelled from across the room. I noticed he had made no move to enter our home. I didn't know what that was about, but I preferred people who exploded my home to stay outside of it, anyway. "So you explode first and then ask if you have the right place? What cut-rate outfit do you work for?"

Emeric remained in the hallway, but I could see his features even clearer now as he formed a white orb of power in one hand near his face. A brief smile crossed his lips as he gazed across the room at me.

"*You* must be Simon Strong," he said and pointed with his free hand. "Impetuous, rude, and clueless. That makes you"—he shifted his gaze to Monty—"Mage Montague, nephew to Dexter Montague, son to Connor Montague of the usurped Golden Circle, oui?"

"My father had nothing to do with the usurping of the Golden Circle," Monty said with a sharp edge. "My uncle acted for reasons he believed to be valid.

"This is true," Emeric said. "Connor Montague was deceased at the time the rogue Montague acted. I meant no insult to your father's memory."

"But you freely call my uncle a rogue?" Monty asked, his words clipped and full of thinly veiled menace. "Measure your next words carefully. I suggest you state the edict and leave the premises."

Emeric narrowed his eyes and stared at Monty.

For a brief moment, I thought Emeric was going to fling the orb he held. His body tensed up and then he relaxed, letting out a short breath as the fake smile returned to his lips.

He didn't absorb the orb though. It still gave off a bright white light as it hovered in his hand next to his face. I could feel the power concentrated in the orb, even from where I stood.

"I see you know the rules," Emeric said with a short nod. "Very well." He cleared his throat and gestured in the air, materializing a series of golden symbols. "So it is written—"

"What does that say?" I asked Monty under my breath. "What is written?"

"That is an official edict," Monty said, still looking at Emeric. "Let him finish."

"Yes, let me finish," Emeric said, giving me a healthy dose of stink-eye. "If you would be so kind."

I waved him on to continue.

"Don't let me stop you," I said. "Nothing stopped you from blowing up our home."

Emeric looked around at the destruction and smiled a little wider. I wanted to use five-knuckle therapy to remove the smirk from his face, but Monty gave me a look and I decided against it...for now.

"From where I am standing, I did you both a favor," Emeric said. "Now you can finish the demolition and build something useful—what do you call it? Ah, yes, a junkyard. A place to keep discarded garbage that has no use."

"Can I shoot him now?"

"No," Monty said, but I could tell he was getting upset. "You have an edict to issue. Do so and exit."

The smirk of satisfaction remained on Emeric's face for a little while longer before he focused on the runes hanging in the air before him and grew serious.

He cleared his throat and began reading while staying outside in the hallway. I was beginning to wonder why he didn't come inside. It was strange behavior to stay outside. I was about to ask Monty when the magistrate began speaking.

"On behalf of Emissary Dubois, I officially declare that as a result of Dexter Montague's unauthorized actions regarding the Golden Circle, an erasure has been sanctioned by the Grand Council. Such erasure is to be executed, not only against the person of Dexter Montague but will also include all living relatives. You will be given twenty-four hours from the time of the pronouncement of this edict to surrender and comply. It has been determined and written by all the members of the Grand Council and hereby fulfilled by Emissary Dubois and Magistrate Emeric."

Emeric looked at his watch.

"Your twenty-four hours begin now," Emeric continued. "Do you have any questions?"

"All living relatives?" I asked, glancing at Monty. "That means you? They want to erase you too?"

Monty nodded.

I turned back to the magistrate who I was disliking more and more by the second. He still had the smug expression of superiority on his face, as if delivering this news was the highlight of his day.

Knowing him, it probably was.

"I have one question," I said.

"Not being a relative, you are not named in the edict," Emeric answered. "If Mage Montague wishes to entertain your question, I will oblige you with an answer, if it is within my power."

"I do," Monty said. "Ask your question, Simon."

"Very well, Mr. Strong," Emeric said with a sigh as if I was wasting his time. "Ask your question."

"What happens if the twenty-four hours pass and no one surrenders?" I asked. "What happens then?"

Emeric narrowed his gaze at me and grew serious. His expression hardened as he looked from me to Monty.

"There are contingencies," he said. "If the edict is not fulfilled, more extreme measures will be implemented."

"More extreme measures, like?"

"The edict will be escalated to E&E—Erasure and Extermination," he said as the brief smile reappeared. For a second, it looked like he hoped we didn't follow the edict. "It would be in your best interests to surrender, no? Erasure is better than death, don't you agree?"

I was fed up with his smug, superior, arrogant ass. I opened the doors to the conference room and stepped out with Peaches by my side. He gave off a low growl as Emeric shot him a wary look, but stood his ground. The man was very brave, very powerful or very stupid.

It didn't matter, I was ending this formality now.

"You think he's going to sit there and let you erase him?" I asked, keeping my rage in check. This magistrate represented everything I disliked about mages and those who wielded power unfairly over others they considered less than. "You must be more brain-damaged than I imagined. No mage in their right mind, especially not a Montague, would volunteer to be erased, not by you or anyone."

"You do speak one truth in your words, Monsieur," he said, his voice full of a quiet menace. "There have been no Montagues who are or have been, in their 'right mind' as you say, for many centuries. This edict is not *optional* and it is not a request. The Grand Council has spoken and its will shall be carried out. If you choose to interfere—"

"You better believe I'm going to interfere," I said, cutting him off. "You think you can come to our home and threaten us?"

"I did not threaten you," Emeric said. "In twenty-four hours, I will return to fulfill the edict. I will be well within my rights to add you to the edict if you choose to interfere. I will not be able to erase you, since you are a pitiful non-mage, but

I can and will eliminate you, and your oversized abomination of a guard dog."

"You should not have said that," Monty said, staring at Emeric. "You have over stepped your position, Magistrate."

"Have I?" The smug smile was back. "I do not think you appreciate how serious your situation is, Mage Montague."

"I fully understand my position," Monty said. "You are the one operating with incomplete information."

Emeric shook his head.

"I advised Emissary Dubois against giving you a grace period, sure that you would not accept your fate honorably, but he refused, being a much bigger man than I."

"On that we agree, you are a huge ass—"

"I would have unleashed the wrath of the Grand Council and brought death to you all, ending this farce," Emeric continued, cutting me off. "I would have leveled this hovel you call a home."

"There are innocents who live in this building."

"How can you be so naive and yet still live in this world?" Emeric mocked. "There is no one who takes breath who is innocent—no one. That you can state so with such certainty only reinforces that you are an ignorant, imprudent child playing with forces you have no capacity to understand. Eliminating you would be a mercy."

"The only one getting eliminated here is you," I said, reaching for Grim Whisper. "I'm going to—"

"Simon, no!" Monty yelled, reaching for my hand. "That gives him reasonable—"

I was fast, but Emeric was faster. As I reached for Grim Whisper, he had released his orb. It crashed into the conference room doors and the world exploded in white light.

NINE

When I could see again, dozens of bright spots danced in my field of vision. Behind the spots stood one very angry-looking TK, staring into my face.

"What exactly were you thinking?" she asked, her voice calm and laced with all the warmth of an arctic winter. "Explain it to me using small words, so there is no misunderstanding between your words and the potential violence I intend to release."

The anger in her voice was the first indicator I was in danger. The fact that she was looking at me with a mild smile and venom in her eyes were the other clues that I may have entered a low-survivability zone.

"What happened?" I asked, looking around the interior of our space. I was lying on the Hansen, which meant I was taking my life into my own hands in more ways than one. "The magistrate hit me with an orb...a white orb of power."

"The magistrate didn't hit you with anything," TK said, still staring at me. "Do you want to know how I know this?"

Before answering, I took stock of the situation I was in. The front door was still a mangled titanium mess and lay in several pieces near the entrance to the conference room. The cool breeze that circulated through our space was courtesy of the new ventilation system provided by our destroyed windows—runed windows, actually—scattered all over our floor in shards.

The conference room doors, which Monty had robustified before Magistrate Limerick unleashed destruction on them, were shredded, with the only parts remaining intact being the hinges, which were still attached to the door frames. I shuddered at the thought of what would've happened to us if Monty hadn't reinforced those doors at the last second.

I was currently lying on the lounge, the one piece of furniture in our home we were expressly forbidden from sitting on, much less laying down on, surrounded by debris and staring up at TK, who, from the look on her face would, if she could, unleash a baleful glare of her own and drill laserbeams into my forehead.

I patted my hand across my chest and took a mental survey of my condition. Everything was attached, so far, though that was subject to change if TK decided to go ballistic. I sensed around the room and found my hellhound quietly munching on a large sausage under the table.

Monty was behind me and to the side.

He was currently having a low conversation on the phone, speaking to someone in a measured but definitely angry tone.

Monty did angry unlike most people.

He was English, after all, and a 'modicum of decorum is to be maintained at all times despite the circumstances one finds themselves in' according to him, even when angry.

Especially when angry.

The way I knew he was angry was that his accent had become more pronounced, and his sentences became shorter and shorter until they became one-word responses. He could go from English-lite to deep Buckingham Palace when he became upset.

I refocused on TK.

One, because ignoring her presence is suicidal, especially when she's staring daggers at your face. And two—well, one is usually enough reason to focus on her when she has her attention on you.

No one ignores TK for long, not if breathing regularly and prolonging your life is on the agenda for the day.

"How *do* you know?" I asked, measuring my words and tone. Considering she was livid, I wasn't eager to send her into homicidal mode. That didn't mean I was going to lay here and let her verbally shred me. Emeric was the one who unleashed the orb. "Are you seeing the damage around here? *He* started it."

"Are you stating this was an unprovoked attack?" TK asked her voice still that faux calm that chilled your blood. "You mean to tell me, the magistrate attacked you with no provocation?"

"It's not like I flung an orb of destruction at him," I said, sitting up and pausing as the floor settled and stopped seesawing. When the world ceased tipping back and forth, I took a deep breath and let it out slowly as I stood. I stepped away from the Hansen, to one of the other chairs in the reception area. "He unleashed the first attack, without us even knowing. He blew out all of the windows, which could've killed us by the way. Do you see those pieces of glass, runed glass? This place was a battlefield. Any one of those pieces could've ended us."

"In theory," she said, glancing at some of the shards buried in the walls, "*you* were never in mortal danger."

"That makes it okay?" I asked. "What about the principle of exploding someone's home without cause or reason?"

"The magistrate does appear to have taken his duties seriously," she said. "A little too seriously."

"Then, he comes to the door, after he explodes our windows, and blasts the door off its hinges," I said. "That thing is titanium. He cut through it and sent the pieces at us. Runed titanium pieces can be deadly, especially at that speed."

She glanced over at what was left of our front door scattered all over the floor, before turning her gaze back to me and nodding in silence.

"Tristan," she said, after a few seconds, without looking at Monty. "At what point did the magistrate enter the premises to inflict bodily harm on you and Strong?"

"He didn't," Monty said, hanging up from his call. "He remained outside the property at all times, as is customary when an edict is being delivered."

"He didn't come inside and threaten either of you?" she asked, looking around at the damage. "All this damage and you didn't feel threatened?"

"I felt threatened," I said. "When my home is turned into a live-fire exercise range, I feel threatened."

"There is always a probability of harm," Monty said, following her gaze with his own. "However in Simon's defense, this is his first time being the recipient of an edict."

"There is that," she said, nodding again. "He had no way of knowing what was going on."

"None," Monty said. "I had no time to brief him on edict protocol. The magistrate arrived and unleashed a succession of concussive blasts."

"Concussive blasts aren't the best choice for perimeter defense neutralization," TK said, looking at where the front door used to be. "Did he at least disable the defenses?"

"Some, but not all," Monty said. "Most of the passive defenses are still in place."

"Disappointing," TK said with a shake of her head. "There was a time when the disabling blast of a magistrate would level entire blocks. The Grand Council has grown soft."

"Soft?" I said pointing to the walls. "You call this going soft?"

"Yes," she said. "It was good that he decided to adhere to the edict delivery protocol, then. He would have had a few nasty surprises if he had chosen to enter and really damage your home."

I stared at her and shook my head.

"Aside from the fact that we were being assaulted," I said, getting upset as I looked around. "You *did* notice all of the destruction?"

"Here is a better question for you," she said. "Why am *I* here? Do you think I was just in the neighborhood and decided to stop by for a visit?"

I gave her question some thought and ran the earlier events through my head, remembering or trying to remember what happened to the best of my ability.

There was nothing in my memory that pointed to summoning TK. As damaging as the destruction was, I didn't feel like I was in any real danger. It could be that I was so used to getting chased, threatened, and attacked that I was getting used to the constant violence in my life.

I hoped not.

I looked around and noticed that TK was alone. LD wasn't here. I stilled and let my senses expand for a few seconds. I only felt Monty, TK, and Peaches. We were the only ones in the space.

"Why *are* you here?" I asked, looking around. "Where's LD?"

"You tell me," she said crossing her arms. "That's not a rhetorical question."

This must've been what Dex meant when he said he informed the Boutique. Whatever damage the magistrate did cause, set something off that brought TK here. Since she was inside the Moscow, making sure we were intact, LD must've been outside checking the perimeter.

"LD is securing the outer defenses," I guessed. "Since you're here, he's making sure the magistrate was alone?"

"Close enough," she said. "Magistrates almost always function as sole operatives. LD will be here shortly to let us know his assessment of any exterior threats."

That was when I noticed, she was in combat armor. The armor was more complex than what she usually wore. Runes were inscribed along certain sections of the armor. The symbols, which I couldn't decipher, pulsed with a green energy as the armor gave off a deep powerful energy signature.

I couldn't tell if the signature was her or the armor, but I didn't want to confront either when I sensed how much power was surrounding her.

"Does that armor enhance your energy signature somehow?" I asked, glancing at the armor. "Does it give you more power?"

She looked down at the armor before looking at me.

"Why do you ask?"

"I know you're strong," I said. "But it feels like you've upgraded your power level."

"This combat armor is a dampener," she said, admiring the armor as she spoke. "It actually masks my energy signature. It provides me with a degree of anonymity. I can mingle with others without attracting too much attention."

"Masks?" I said incredulously. "Are you saying you're stronger than what I'm sensing?"

"Simon..." Monty said, giving me a look and shaking his head. "Your questions are inappropriate. If you can't determine her energy signature from scanning with your innersight then you shouldn't—"

"Let him," TK said looking directly at me. "He needs to learn. Scan me with your innersight. Use it fully. I'll remove the barriers in the armor."

I glanced at Monty who wore an expression of controlled dislike for this whole idea, as if someone had just exchanged his tea with Death Wish and forgot to tell him about it.

"Are you sure?" I asked. "I'm not breaking some mage code of conduct that's going to get me in trouble?"

"You have somehow managed to get the Grand Council's attention," she said with a small smile. "I think you have filled the allotted quota for trouble one person can achieve."

"Is that a yes or a no?"

"Scan and we will see what you see," she said. "This will be a good lesson for you."

"A good lesson?" I asked. "How is this a good lesson?"

She crossed her arms and stared at me.

"Fine," I said, interpreting her silence as permission. "This better not melt my brain."

"In order for that to occur, you would need to be in possession of one," she said. "Stop stalling and unleash your full innersight."

"Are you sure that's wise?" Monty asked, concerned. "He's competent, but he hasn't mastered its use."

"I will prevent the brain-melting," she said. "This will be good for him. He needs to master this skill, especially if he is going to work with Badb Catha."

The mention of her name made my body shudder reflexively.

"What do you mean?"

"I will explain...after you perform the scan," she said. "Ready?"

"Not really?"

"Good," she said, gesturing. "Determine my energy level. You have five seconds."

"Five seconds?"

"Four now."

I closed my eyes and let my senses expand.

I was immediately blasted back by a wave of power washing over my body. It overwhelmed me, nearly driving me to my knees. I suddenly felt too heavy; even standing was a struggle. I forced my eyes open and blinded myself. An explosion of green energy blazed around TK like the corona of a sun.

It was impossible to stare at her for more than a fraction of a second. I quickly turned my face away to avoid really blinding myself. Even now, the after-image of the brief moment I managed was burned into my eyes.

A few seconds later, the wave of power vanished.

I peeked open an eye and saw Monty and TK looking at me.

"Well?" TK asked. "What did you manage to understand?"

"Your energy level is over nine-thousand?"

"He doesn't understand," Monty said. "He doesn't have a context."

"Then I will provide him with one," she said in a way that made me wary as she turned to me. "You have an understanding with Badb Catha, correct?"

"I do."

"Do you understand what that means?"

"Not really," I said honestly. "I'm supposed to go work for her—"

"Kill," she said. "You will become the Morrigan's Hand. You will kill for her."

"Kill for her?"

"It is what you agreed to," she said. "Were you unclear as to the conditions of your assistance?"

"I knew I had to go work for her, I didn't think—"

"Truly?" TK asked. "What did you think 'work for her' meant? What kind of work did you think she would have you do? Some odd jobs around her house? Some plumbing, maybe some light carpentry, or a little painting?"

"Well, no, I mean, it's just—"

"You knew," she said, her tone certain. "Deep inside, you knew what it meant and you accepted the arrangement, conditionally, but you accepted. Yes?"

I nodded.

"Yes," I said. "I formed the final terms of the agreement. She agreed to the pact."

"Fifty years of service, with autonomy and veto power?" she said. "As far as pacts go, you did well, overall. Still, Badb Catha is ancient. You could not have covered all the angles."

"I know," I said. "But I have the option when I start."

"You only think you do," TK said, shaking her head. "What if Tristan is suddenly struck by some obscure mage illness? Or Cece and Peanut, who are not immortal like you, find themselves in mortal danger? What if your hellhound is attacked and needs assistance beyond what you can provide?"

"Then I will—"

"Do whatever you must to keep them safe."

"Yes," I said. "I would."

"Now, think of the multitude whose lives are touched by yours," she said. "Any one of them can be used to leverage you into service."

"I make the choice when I start."

"You think you have a choice as to when you start?" she asked. "You're wrong. That choice is an illusion. She is allowing you the luxury of thinking you have control, but she wields the control in this dynamic, always has and always will."

"How did you do it?"

TK looked away for a few seconds before turning back to face me.

"I served my time."

"But you escaped, you got away, how?"

"I will tell you, but we will have to discuss your pact in the future," she said. "You have no idea what you will be facing. That is a conversation for another time."

"I'll do what I have to, because I gave my word," I said. "That doesn't mean I have to like it."

"Good, we're being honest. Now to give you some context," she said. "You sensed a fraction of my power."

"A fraction?"

"Yes, a fraction, what your brain could withstand without melting," she said, glancing at Monty, then back at me. "Here is your context. The power you just experienced will be achieved by Tristan in five hundred to a thousand years, if he trains hard."

"A thousand?"

"If he hits the shifts he needs to hit, and has a little help along the way."

"That long?"

"Possibly longer," she answered. "The power I currently possess is dwarfed by the Morrigan by several orders of magnitude," she continued. "If I manage to live for several millennia, I could hope to approach a fraction of her power, the same way you could achieve a fraction of Kali's power as her Marked."

I stood there in mild shock.

"The only difference between us, is that you might actually live long enough to attain that level of power," she continued. "For greater context, and to give you some semblance of comprehension why this is all happening, Dexter is one of the few mages alive that has achieved a level of power that presents a threat to a being like the Morrigan."

"What?" I asked. "He's that powerful?"

"Yes," TK said. "Now, why am I here?"

"Dex reached out to the Boutique—Fordey Boutique."

"Yes, why else?" she asked. "Think to what I just told you about your pact."

I gave her words some thought.

The Grand Council was angry with Dex, that was for sure, but they weren't strong enough to go up against him directly. He was too strong and he had no vulnerabilities, unless going around exposing yourself to people was a weakness I didn't know about.

He did have vulnerabilities.

The same way I had vulnerabilities.

Suddenly I saw it.

Think of the multitude whose lives are touched by yours. Any one of them can be used to leverage you into service.

It dawned on me with a frigid realization.

We were Dex's weakness.

Monty, me, Peaches, Cece, Peanut, and anyone else Dex called his family. Anyone he cared about could be used against him.

Was the Grand Council that determined? Were they that insane? Even worse, were they that suicidal to risk pissing off Dex by going after those closest to him?

I didn't have to look far for the answer to that question, I was standing in the blown-apart reception area of my home. They were more than willing. They were determined to force Dex's hand into surrendering to an erasure by threatening Monty.

TEN

"You understand why I am here, now," she said with a brief nod.

"*We're* his vulnerability," I said piecing it together as Monty nodded, his expression grim. "They will come after Monty—"

"And you," TK added. "You two are the weak links in Dex's life."

"What about Cece and Peanut?" I asked, feeling slightly offended. "They are both—"

"Being guarded by the Morrigan," TK finished. "I'd hazard the Grand Council will think twice about going after those two children. To even attempt it would be a death sentence. No, the Grand Council will stick to targets of opportunity."

"Which means us," Monty said. "They will use the relocation of the Golden Circle as a pretense to carry out their agenda of removing my uncle…permanently."

"Dex really knows how to make enemies," I said. "Why do they hate him so much?"

"Live long enough and you will make dangerous enemies,"

TK answered. "They hate him for several reasons, what he is doing with those children being chief among them. He is creating a new generation of battlemages."

"I thought that would be a good thing?" I said. "New battlemages are good, right?"

"Conditionally," TK explained. "To the Grand Council, it would only be a good thing, if *they* were the ones creating the battlemages, because that would mean—"

"They would control them," I finished. "This is the active warfare Monty mentioned."

"Yes," TK added. "From their perspective, no one trains up battlemages unless they're preparing for war. They aren't only livid about Dex borrowing the Golden Circle. The deeper reason, the reason for the Emissary, is that they view his actions as an act of aggression."

"An aggression," I said. "Against who?"

"Doesn't matter," TK said. "Training battlemages is the same as raising an army, in this case a magical army capable of immense destruction, controlled by an insanely powerful mage who isn't exactly a fan of the Grand Council."

"Won't that make them go after Peanut and Cece even more?"

"They won't," Monty said. "They *will* come after us. Right now, we present the softest targets to them. which is why the edict was issued."

TK nodded.

"So far," she said with an evil smile. "They don't exactly know about Dex's involvement with the Ten. To attack one, is to attack all."

"So it is true. Dex is really part of the Ten?" I asked still surprised. "I thought you never wanted him in the Ten, he was too reckless."

"The Ten embody the outcast," TK said. "It's ironic that

the cast out gathered together to form a group of their own—a group of outcasts."

"That motto doesn't apply to Monty and me," I said. "We're not members of the Ten. We're not even honorary members."

"Not yet."

"Not yet?" I said, glancing at Monty. "Did you speak to her?"

"No, I have not," Monty said.

"Then how did she—?"

"I sent a formal request for inclusion into the Ten after we dealt with Esti and her Demogre. It was my uncle who brought up the topic of Caligo and Rakta—Caligo's master."

"We're not ready for Caligo or those who control her," I said. "What did Dex say about her?"

"He said more or less what you just said. At our current power levels, we are not ready to face Caligo, her master, or the entities within those circles of power," Monty said. "He said he knew a way to get us ready, but it would be a painful and torturous path."

"Because why would it be easy and pain-free?"

"Indeed," Monty said. "His proposed method is somewhat unorthodox, to say the least."

"The Ten," I said, glancing at TK, and I knew it to be true. "Dex was the one who suggested we join the Ten?"

"Yes," Monty said, glancing at TK. "We will have to be initiated into the Order of the Ten."

I looked at TK.

"Do we have a chance?"

"Slim," she said. "But it's the only one you have to face what's coming for you. You need to become stronger—both of you."

"What happens if we fail this initiation?"

"You die," TK said matter-of-factly. "Not today, but

without the Ten, you will lack the weapons and defenses you will need to fight the Grand Council, Caligo, and those who stand in the shadows controlling her."

I felt like all this time I had been wading in the shallow end of the magical pool. I didn't realize that the floor of this particular pool was sloped with a severe drop-off at one end.

At the moment, it felt as if I had stepped from the relatively safe but occasionally lethal, three-foot deep section to the instantaneously toxic, life-ending Mariana Trench side of the pool.

I was in way over my head.

I heard my hellhound rumble in the kitchen.

Peaches padded over to where I sat and slapped me in the face with his enormous tongue. He moved so fast, I didn't have a chance to react before I was soaked with healing saliva.

I tried pushing him away from me, but failed to budge him more than a few inches. I stared at his immense head and realized that due to his current diet, he had gotten so heavy that moving him without a specialized hellhound crane was becoming impossible. I did manage to create some space between us, just enough to prevent another lightning tongue-lashing.

<My saliva will heal you, bondmate.>

<I don't need healing right now. If I get hurt, I will definitely go for the slobber first-aid. Right now we have bad people coming after us.>

<Can I bite them?>

<I don't want biting to be the first solution to everything. How about using your baleful glare or speaking to them with your powerful bark? Why biting?>

<Biting lets me stop them right away. I never miss when I bite.>

He did make a good point.

<Okay, that makes sense, but how about we wait a bit first before

we start biting. That way I can figure out how dangerous these people will be. I don't want you facing something that could hurt you.>

<There are few things that could hurt me. I am a hellhound and I eat plenty of meat.>

<Still, as indestructible as you are, let's not take the chance and rush into dangerous situations without finding out what we're facing. You wait for my go-ahead before attacking or biting. Fair enough?>

<I will wait for you before attacking. We are bondmates, we will fight together.>

<Thanks, I just don't want you getting hurt.>

"What is the grace period?" TK asked, heading to the armory with Monty and me in tow. "How long did the Grand Council give you?"

"Twenty-four hours," Monty said. "Which is standard, or so I've been informed."

"Terms of the edict?"

"Erasure for my uncle, me, and any other living relatives of the Montague lineage," Monty said. "Which means—"

"Just Dex and you," she said. "That whole family of direct lineage clause is an excuse to erase you both. They have no other Montagues to chase at the moment. Besides, it's Dex that they want. You're a target of convenience. Did they mention Strong?"

Monty nodded.

"At first it was only if he interfered," Monty said, glancing at me and shaking his head. "He was not included in the edict, not being a Montague or a mage."

"And Strong decided to remain silent, watching from the sidelines and absorbing everything he could about the magistrate," TK said. "In fact, I'm guessing Strong played it weak to draw no attention to himself. He acted like an innocent bystander, right?"

"Not exactly," Monty answered. "Simon decided that

violence was the correct response to the edict. As you can see, Emeric had a direct response for him."

"I see," she said, glancing around at the wreckage. "What exactly prompted this response?"

"You mean besides the magistrate kindly redecorating our home in modern warzone, and then offering to erase and eliminate Monty?" I said. "Then on top of blowing up my home, he dumps all over it, as if I live in a trash heap and I'm not fit to wipe the shit from his shoe."

"You've had enemies offer you worse," she said, turning to me. "What was different this time?"

I stared at her and flexed my jaw, letting the anger come off me in controlled waves.

I knew who I was talking to.

TK was a major threat, but I wasn't scared of her. I respected the power she wielded because she didn't come across as some pampered mage who learned her craft by studying books in some sect's stuffy room.

Dex and Monty had both shared enough clues for me to understand that she earned her power in the trenches, working with the Morrigan and suffering for the privilege.

That was part of what made her so intimidating. The rest of it was that although she wasn't nearly as strong, from what I could tell, as Dex or the Morrigan, she did command their respect.

"He came to my *home*, tore it apart, called it trash, threatened Dex and Monty, *my family*," I said, then gave it some more thought. "Then he said the one thing he shouldn't have."

"Which was?" she asked, the smile returning to her face. "What triggered you?"

"He promised to eliminate me, which if I had a dollar for every time someone threatened to wipe me off the face of the earth, I'd have a nice-sized account by now, but he took it too far." I glanced at my massive hellhound. "He threatened to eliminate my oversized *abomination of a guard dog.*"

"I see," TK said rubbing Peaches' enormous head. "And you responded with?"

"Simon tried to shoot the magistrate," Monty answered. "Emeric constituted that act as willful disregard of the edict and amended the targets to include Simon."

"Pretense," TK said. "They were always coming after you two, three. Now they have a valid reason. Tristan, what kind of cast did the magistrate use in response? Did you get a moment to analyze it?

"Concussive cast," Monty said. "Strong enough to require me to create several shields to deflect and dissipate most of the force from the blast."

"They were always coming after us?" I said in mild surprise. "They were?"

"You're still not seeing it? Really?"

"No, I'd prefer someone illuminate me," I said, getting fed up with people trying to remove me from situations or reduce my lifespan to zero. "I'm not seeing it, no. All I'm seeing is enemies trying to exterminate me for standing in their way."

TK nodded.

"Who do you think pulls Verity's strings?" TK asked as she filled a bag with ammunition for Grim Whisper. "Same with Penumbra overseas. The Grand Council sits in the shadows and orders others to kill, blackmail, and destroy. All while claiming to do the necessary work the sects won't or can't do."

"They're really coming in twenty-four hours?"

"No," she said, looking at her watch. "Don't be naïve. What makes you think they would keep their word to you? They have already condemned you to erasure and death."

"But the magistrate—?"

"Said what he was told to say," she said, pulling out a phone. "Sanitizers are on their way even as we speak."

"He lied," I said, offended. "The twenty-four-hour grace period is to catch us off guard. He wants us to drop our guard and to lull us into a false sense of security."

"Yes," Monty said. "We would think we had a full twenty-four hours when it's closer to two, or less."

"Less," TK said, pressing a button on her phone. "I have them. Exfil in five minutes. Any activity on the perimeter?"

"The Sanitation company has several vehicles headed our way," LD said over the phone. "I can engage them, but the old man gave us specific instructions. Still, it would be fun to—"

"No, we stick to the plan, darling," TK said. "You can play all you want with them, once we get these three safe. Dex would be livid if we placed them in harm's way unnecessarily."

"True," LD said. "Hola hombres. Things just got real so no sugarcoating. Grand Council has a vendetta for Dex and is taking it out on you two. No, it's not fair, but it's life. We make do. Get your asses out of there now. See you on the other side."

He hung up before I had a chance to say anything.

"The Grand Council has no honor."

"Imagine that, a corrupt organization lying to its intended victims," she said, tossing me the bag. "Tristan, grab any magical artifacts that are important to you. You two won't be back here any time soon."

"They've been packed away for some time."

"Good," TK said. "Only thing left to do is to fix this mess."

"All of the windows and the door are destroyed," I said. "I don't even think Monty can fix this anytime soon. The windows were runed along with the door. Olga is going to lose her mind; she hates it when the Moscow gets damaged."

Monty nodded.

"Given enough time, I could restore them all," Monty said. "However, time is a luxury we don't currently enjoy."

"Your Landlady has an understanding with Dex," TK said, tracing some complicated symbols in the air. "She realizes that Dex is keeping Cece safe at the school. As for the damage, it's resolved."

I had never seen these symbols and the runes glowed a bright green while they hovered in the center of the reception area.

"This doesn't look resolved," I said. "It looks like we had a minor battle in here."

Monty stepped close to the hovering symbols, and I could tell he had entered professor mode from the look in his eyes. He muttered some words of surprise under his breath as he examined them up close.

"Is that Ziller's Formula of Temporal Permutation?" Monty asked, inspecting the hovering symbols. "Professor Ziller himself said this was impossible to trace out runically. There are symbols here I never saw in the original teachings."

"Some of the components were deliberately omitted," TK said as she headed to the entrance. "Can't have any of those first-year teleportation mages attempting a cast of this level and teleporting themselves to an early grave."

"Does this really do what I think—?"

"Door," she said, pointing to the exit. "Did I mention Sanitizers were on their way?"

We headed to the door as TK swept an arm through the air, sending a wave of green energy into the hovering runic symbols while whispering something to herself.

The symbols transformed, becoming a bright blue-green before turning a brilliant white and blinding us as we stood at the entrance.

When the light dimmed, the door was in one piece and

back in its frame. She pushed it slightly, peeked inside, and checked the windows. There was no glass on the floor and all the windows were intact.

"How did—?" I started and stopped as I took in our space. It was in perfect condition. "Everything is fixed. How did you manage to fix—?"

"Later," she said moving down the hall and taking the stairs to the garage. "We need to move—now. Let's go."

ELEVEN

We arrived at the garage level several minutes later.

I arrived at the door before anyone else and made to open the door but Peaches clamped his massive jaw around my leg and pulled.

"Whoa!" I said as he shook his head, yanking me to the side, away from the door. "What are you doing?"

His action caused me to pull on the handle, opening the door. Monty extended his hand, causing a blast of air to finish shoving me out of the way.

I looked on in surprise as a large black orb of energy flew past, narrowly missing me and slamming into the wall opposite the door.

"Saving your life, apparently," TK said, glancing at Peaches. "It seems they anticipated you using the car."

"What the—?" I managed. "That orb looked deadly."

She pointed to the wall where the orb had impacted. It had begun melting the concrete of the wall into a sludge that pooled on the floor.

That sludge slowly began eating at the floor, forming a

small crater filled with superacid. Seconds later, the crater became a hole that the superacid disappeared down.

"Sanitizers," TK said, the word a curse. "They're early."

"What the hell was that?" I asked still looking at the hole. "They're flinging orbs of acid?"

"It's the equivalent of runic fluroantimonic acid," she said. "That cast will melt you in seconds."

"Sanitizers employ venomancers in their ranks it seems," Monty said. "This will complicate things."

"You faced one with Verity and the Wordweavers," TK said. "Above Verity and the High Tribunal, sit the Grand Council. They are the ultimate authority in the magical community. Only they would have authorized their use."

"I remember Edith," I said. "I remember how much fun venomancers were, as she tried to kill us."

Monty glanced at the hole in the concrete.

"It would appear these are advanced," he said. "Runic acid takes several of its properties from a rare poison. Even among their ranks, this is not common knowledge."

"They better not melt the Dark Goat," I said. "I will be pissed if the car gets melted...again."

"Let's address the priorities," TK said. "First the acid, then the venomancers."

TK gestured and several green orbs followed the superacid down the hole. I looked down at Peaches and rubbed his head in appreciation.

<*Thank you, boy. That would've hurt.*>

<*The bad smelling people were waiting for us.*>

<*You smelled them?*>

<*Yes, but they were hiding. I could not smell them enough.*>

<*I didn't sense them at all. They were hiding well.*>

<*You didn't smell them because you need to eat more meat like me. When you become stronger, no one will be able to hide from us.*>

<Are you saying if I get stronger, you get stronger? Is that how this works?>

<We are bondmates. I am very strong, but I have to wait for you to get stronger to show all my strength. When you get stronger, I will show you more of my strength.>

Call me slow to the party, but it was finally beginning to click. As my power increased, more of Peaches' abilities would be revealed. The stronger I became, the stronger *we* became.

I could understand a bit more about why hellhounds and their bondmates were so feared. If I became powerful, an immortal bondmate with his hellhound...shit.

We would be unstoppable.

No wonder people wanted to kill us now, while we were still relatively weak.

I really needed to pay Hades a visit.

"We need to use the other exit," I said. "I'm sure they have that one covered too, but if they think we are here, we can surprise them and get to the Dark Goat before they have a chance to recover."

"Sounds like a solid plan," TK said. "I have a variation if you don't mind."

I raised my hands in surrender and stepped back.

"I don't mind at all," I said. "I'm not exactly eager to step out into acid orb central. If your plan can stop them from trying to disintegrate us, I'm all for it."

The energy around TK intensified and I saw Monty take a step back, concern on his face. He gave me a look that said: *Give her plenty of room. Whatever she's about to unleash is going to be nasty and lethal.*

I stepped back another step and stood closer to Monty. It may have looked like I was stepping away from TK in fear, but really what I was doing was giving her room to do whatever it was she was going to do.

Also, I sensed the energy spike around her and fear played a part, a small part, in giving her extra room. TK focused on the door and began to gesture.

All around her, black energy began to coalesce. Her usual green signature in things was absent. This energy felt dark and dangerous.

Peaches whined as he stepped closer to my leg and nearly bumped me into the wall.

<*The scary lady feels scary. Her energy smells like home.*>
<*Smells like home? What does that mean?*>
<*It doesn't smell alive. She is calling death.*>

I turned to focus on TK again and the energy around her began taking form. All around her, I started seeing ravens. Normally, this would throw me, well, it did. TK didn't make it a habit to walk around with a flock of ravens, but it kind of made sense considering who her mentor was.

The other uncanny thing was that these ravens were just floating in the air. There was no flapping of wings, and they were completely silent. All of them had bright red eyes and some of them were focused on me.

It creeped me out how they turned their heads to get a better look at me. Monty looked warily in my direction, his face fixed in a grim expression.

"I thought only the Morrigan could summon an unkindness," Monty said carefully. "This is unprecedented."

"Who do you think taught me this cast?" TK said. "I don't appreciate orbs of acid flung in my direction. Once I unleash them, do not stop moving. Head for your car and exit the garage."

"What are you going to do?"

"I'm going to deal with the Sanitizers," she said and for a brief moment, I felt pity for the Sanitizers in the garage. They were all dead, they just didn't know it yet. "If I don't stop these here, they will pursue you, and we can't have that... not yet."

"Not yet?" I asked. "Does that mean—?"

"LD will meet up with you once you leave the garage," she said cutting me off. "He will escort you to the next rendezvous point."

"You're not coming?" I asked. "At all?"

"Don't be so dramatic, Strong," she said with an evil smile. "I'll meet up with you all later, if I can. There is more happening here than you can see. The priority is to make sure you three get through this in one piece."

There were easily ten to fifteen ravens floating around her in that eerie disturbing way of non-flapping hovering. One of the ravens turned its head and stared right at me.

"Death's Hand," was squawked at me. "Kali's Death Hand."

I looked at it in shock.

"What did you say?" I asked stepping close. "What did you call me?"

"Strong," TK said. "Focus. Reinforcements will be coming. We can't be here when they arrive."

I stepped back and nodded, glancing at Monty who was still looking at the raven who had called me Death's Hand. Monty shook his head and gave me a look that said: *drop it*.

I nodded again and took a deep breath, before letting it out slowly.

I looked at TK.

"I'm ready," I said. "Do what you have to do."

"Give them ten seconds once I release them," she said. "Then head for the car. Do not deviate, do not engage the ravens or the Sanitizers. Focus on the vehicle and head there; that goes for all three of you. Understood?"

Monty and I nodded as Peaches let out a low rumble.

"Good," TK continued. "Move away from the door."

We did as instructed and she slashed her arm downward.

The ravens, as one, flew out the door in a silent flock of death.

A few seconds later, I sensed the orbs being created and heard them sizzling as the acid hit the walls. A few seconds after that, the ravens started cawing or something really close to it.

Then it became silent.

I took a step toward the door and TK placed a hand on my shoulder. I looked at her and she shook her head.

"Wait."

Five seconds passed, and then the screams started.

TWELVE

"Go, now!" TK said, as she stepped out into the garage. "Get to the Abyss. LD will meet you there. Do not stop anywhere else. Clear?"

"Clear," I said, as I ran out into the garage to a scene that would rob me of sleep for many nights to come. "What the actual fu—?"

I came to a standstill as the horror all around me stunned my brain.

"Move, Strong!" TK yelled, with a shove to my back. "Get to the car, unless you want to join them! Go!"

We made it to the Dark Goat as ravens clouded the interior of the garage. I could've sworn only ten to fifteen had exited the stairwell, but now all around us, all I saw were ravens.

Bloody lethal ravens.

The Sanitizers...there was no way they could have prepared for something like this. The ravens mercilessly clawed and gouged at them easily ripping flesh from bone. What was scarier was that the ravens seemed to phase in and out of the plane as they attacked, similar to how Peaches blinked.

Monty was already strapped in by the time I turned on the engine with a roar. I noticed more Sanitizer reinforcements had teleported into the garage, but it only meant more victims for the unkindness of ravens.

Monty's expression was grim as the engine roared to life.

"Get us out of here, Simon," he said. "This is only going to get worse."

"How can it possibly get worse?" I said, flooring the gas and screeching out of the garage. "I've never seen anything like that. Not even in London was it this bad."

I swerved the Dark Goat around the columns in the garage as the screams followed us up the ramp, the sounds of agony burning into my mind.

"That was a different kind of unkindness," Monty said, glancing behind us. "This is...this is different. I can't believe the Morrigan taught her this cast. I can't believe she would actually use it."

"Which *she* are we referring to?"

"TK," he said, still looking behind us. "That cast is not an explosive cast like the one we saw in London with the feathers. This is different, this cast is classified as a purge, and I never thought I would actually see one enacted."

"A purge?" I asked. "As in an evacuation?"

"As in destroying everything in the vicinity," Monty said. "Those ravens will get rid of every living thing on the lower garage level as long as TK commands them."

"*Every* living thing?" I said, as the realization dawned on me. "What are you looking for? There's no one behind us."

"That," he said as he pointed behind us. Peaches whined again and I sensed the power flow over us. "You need to go faster, Simon. Much faster."

I dared a look into the rear-view mirror and for a

moment, there was a disconnect between my brain and my eyes. There behind us was a cloud of black feathers. When I focused and looked closer, I realized it wasn't exactly a cloud of feathers.

It was an immense flock of ravens.

"Monty, why is there a renegade flock of ravens behind us?" I asked, accelerating the Dark Goat even more. "What did TK unleash?"

"As I said, a purge," Monty said. "The myths state that when the dead are on the battlefield, the Morrigan releases this purge to cleanse the dead bodies from the field."

"This purge?" I asked, narrowly dodging another column and getting on the ramp to reach the street level. "The one that's behind us is going to cleanse the garage? What about TK?"

"I'm certain she will be fine," he said, gesturing and forming a large lattice of violet energy behind us. "Whatever you do, do not let those ravens catch up to us."

He released the lattice and it floated behind us, hovering in the center of the ramp. In moments, it spread out and filled the entire space of the ramp. A few moments later, the ravens crashed into the lattice.

The lattice held for all of three seconds, and then it burst apart as the ravens flew through it. For a few more seconds, they were gaining on us, then I saw them slow down. In the middle of the flock, I could just make out a figure surrounded in green energy.

TK.

She walked to the front of the flock, watched us leave the garage, and then headed back down the ramp, the flock of ravens following her.

I wasn't really sure that it was TK or some other entity that would've unleashed feathered death on us, but she looked scarier than usual surrounded by the ravens.

It gave me a moment of pause.

Is that what was going to happen to me when I went to work with the Morrigan? Would proximity to Badb Catha turn me into some kind of monster?

"Monty," I said when my heart had settled back down to three hundred beats a minute. "What would've happened if those ravens had caught up to us? Could you have stopped them?"

"No," he said. "We are stepping into a different realm of power. You saw how effective my lattice was against them."

"Not very," I said, getting onto 10th Avenue. "I think I want this ride to stop. I want to get off."

"There's no getting off," Monty said, voicing my worst fears. "We're on this ride until the end."

"Would they have clawed through the Dark Goat?"

"I honestly don't know what would have happened, and I don't think I want to know," he said. "Cecil has runed this vehicle extraordinarily well, but I don't think he planned for unearthly ravens as a contingency. I'm not eager to find out."

"Me either."

"We best accept that we are facing levels of power we are not prepared to face," he said. "Even with all my years of experience, this is beyond me."

"I hate it when you're being honest," I said. "Are you sure we can't go pay Hades a visit?"

"Absolutely certain," he said. "The Abyss is not far. I have to assume Grey is expecting us, along with LD."

"Wait a second," I said, as a thought struck me. "Is Grey part of the Ten?"

"No," Monty said. "The Night Wardens are forbidden from being members of magical clandestine organizations."

"Aren't the Night Wardens a magical clandestine organization?" I asked, dodging a near collision with one of my city's finest yellow taxi drivers. "They don't exactly advertise, do they?"

"The Night Wardens do not operate as a clandestine organization," Monty explained. "They don't *advertise* their presence, no, but they don't go out of their way to hide from the authorities or beings intent on causing harm to the populace."

"So they're hiding in plain sight?"

"They're not hiding at all," he said. "If you need to find them, you can. Unlike the Ten. You don't find the Ten, they find you."

I noticed the black van trailing us several cars back. Every time I switched a lane, it would wait a few seconds and then do the same. All of the windows were tinted, and I couldn't get a clear look at the driver.

I took a deep breath and focused, letting my senses expand.

I felt Monty next to me through the stormblood. Peaches was even stronger through our bond, and fainter, but just as present, was whoever was in the van behind us and was now one car back.

The energy signature was familiar, not friendly but familiar, the way a punch to the face is a familiar sensation. Not exactly welcome, but not unknown either.

"We have a tail," I said ."It reads like the—"

"Magistrate," Monty said, glancing behind us. "He was waiting for us to exit the Moscow."

"Why didn't he go nuclear in the building?" I asked, swerving around another car. The van followed me smoothly. "We were easy targets there."

"Not exactly," Monty said, as he began gesturing. "They have to adhere to some rules of engagement. Destroying Olga's building would have serious repercussions. The damage created was superficial, some windows and a door—easily repaired."

I nodded.

"If they tried to take us down in the Moscow, they would need to go full attack mode," I said. "I don't think the building would survive that, at least not much of it."

"Precisely," Monty said. "It would bring them undue attention and Olga is not without recourse. She would have been well within her rights to dispatch the magistrate and Sanitizers with extreme prejudice for destroying her property."

"Are you saying they waited for us because they didn't want to piss Olga off?"

"A prudent course of action and something for us to consider as we deal with this situation," he said, releasing small golden orbs out the window. "We won't have much, if any, assistance, but we can hamper the Grand Council's attacks."

"I'm not putting any innocent bystanders in the way," I said, firmly. "Zero collateral damage."

"Agreed," Monty said. "The Abyss should be safe since LD will be there waiting for us and Grey is practically a fringe member of society as it stands."

"Grey," I said. "Are we bringing death to his door? Or should I try and shake the magistrate?"

"No," Monty said. "Head straight for the Abyss."

"That sentence doesn't exactly fill me with any sort of joy," I said. "I'd like to avoid the abyss if at all possible."

"I'm afraid it's too late for that," Monty said. "We have stepped over the edge and are fully in an abyss of sorts."

I glanced at him for a second and shook my head.

"Do mages get anti-morale-building training?" I asked. "Because it really sounds like you are trained to see the worst side of everything."

"Mages are realists," he said. "We see the world as it is,

not as we wish it to be. The sooner you adopt this way of being—"

"The sooner I'll be depressed, sheesh," I said. "You know, there *is* joy in the world. Not that it visits us, but I have heard of it. I know it exists, somewhere, out there."

"Of course it does," Monty said. "The world is not entirely bleak and darkness, bereft of all hope and happiness."

"There you go," I said, with a quick nod. "See? There's hope. It's not all bad and—"

"It's not for us and those like us, who walk mostly in the dark," he continued, cutting me off. "The stark reality of the brutality of life is our constant companion so that others may experience and thrive in this joy you mention. There is always a cost."

"Do we have to be the ones to pay it?"

"Someone has to pay it," he said, looking out his window. "Better it be us, who have some inkling as to what occurs in the shadows than those who are oblivious."

"It's not fair."

"No, but it is just."

"Just unfair if you ask me," I said, glancing in the rear-view mirror. "I can shake them."

He glanced behind us and shook his head.

"No, TK instructed us to go the Abyss," he said. "We go straight there. I have a feeling our tail will think twice about following us inside."

"Why would TK send us to Grey?"

"It actually makes perfect sense. The Dive would be expected, whereas the Grand Council would refrain from attempting to breach the defenses at the Abyss."

"The Grand Council won't attacking us there, really?"

"They're not desperate," Monty said. "With the edict issued, most of our resources will refuse to assist us in this situation."

"That was probably the plan," I said. "Remove our options and then corner us."

"Or so they think," he said. "They will find out we have more options than they imagined, however, if the magistrate fails in his duty—"

"They call the whole thing off?"

"Not even remotely likely," he said, glancing behind us again. "The Emissary will take matters into his own hands. We must be prepared for that eventuality."

"Why does that sound like a worst-case scenario?"

"Because it is," Monty said. "We can't take the Emissary lightly. He is a powerful mage, stronger than either of us individually."

"What about together?" I asked. "Can we take him together?"

"I…I don't know," he said, after a pause. "I'm hoping a conversation with Grey and LD can answer that question."

"The Abyss is up ahead and our tail is giving us some space."

"For now," Monty said. "Let's see how long that patience lasts. Park near the rear."

THIRTEEN

We arrived at the Whitney Museum of Art.

I pulled around to the back of the building and was treated to a level of ugly that made me pause and shake my head.

"This is a building that doesn't know what it wants to be," I said, as I pulled up close to the rear entrance. "Is it a museum or an eyesore?"

"I'd say a bit of both," Monty replied, glancing at the building. "Leaning heavily on the latter."

"Only the Tate is uglier than this…this, I want to say building, but really it's a mistake disguised as a building. What is it with these modern museums being hideous? What's the plan? Make the exterior hurt your eyes so bad that you're actually grateful for what passes as 'art' inside?"

"Park near the rear exit," Monty said, pointing ahead before glancing behind us. "The Abyss has a reputation, but the Grand Council may believe they are beyond the need to observe any rules of engagement."

"Didn't they demonstrate that at the Moscow?"

"No, actually," Monty said. "They were well within their operational parameters as long as they repaired or compensated Olga for the damage they caused."

"You're kidding?"

"I don't kid," Monty said. "This is a different scenario. They may attack us if we extend our time outside the property."

"The less time on the street the better?"

"In this instance, yes," Monty answered. "Let's give them the smallest window of opportunity to attack us."

"They could always just attack us *inside*," I said. "What's to stop them from going *that* route?"

"You mean besides the powerful darkmage who owns this building?" Monty said. "I'd say Grey and his blade is deterrent enough for now. I highly doubt the Grand Council wants an angry Night Warden retaliating for damage to his property."

"Especially not one bonded to a bloodthirsty goddess."

"They will wait for a better opportunity."

I nodded and turned off the Dark Goat's engine. The black van had stopped about a block away and parked catty-corner to the rear entrance. I could hear their engine running.

"They're staying ready," I said, getting out, but keeping my gaze on the van. "Just in case we make a quick exit?"

Monty nodded.

"Do you recall what the Ghost did to our last Goat?"

"It's not like I can forget my vehicle being melted before my eyes," I said as anger rose at the memory. I flexed the muscles of my jaw. "Do you think that Ghost was connected to the Grand Council? He used acid orbs too."

"It's quite possible," Monty said.

"You know, I could go over and shoot the magistrate now," I said, letting my hand drift to Grim Whisper. "Sort of a preemptive preservation of Dark Goat. I am not letting them melt my car again."

"They won't, at least not without us in it," he said as Peaches desprawled and jumped out of the car, causing it to see-saw back and forth before he landed on the sidewalk. "They will bide their time...within reason."

I took a step back, risked my vision, and looked up at the building which housed both the Whitney Museum and below it, unknown to most, the Abyss.

We were standing on the corner of 10th Avenue and Washington Street, with Gansevoort Street to the south and Little West 12th to the north. The Whitney looked more like an industrial factory than a museum.

The Tate took the prize for most hideous looking museum on the planet, but the Whitney was a close second. Modern art museums were just fugly or as Monty recently put it, aesthetically challenged.

"I'm going to have some words with Grey," I said. "I'm sure if this building suffered some major catastrophe, say a hellhound going on a rampage, he could rebuild it and make it look appealing the second time around."

"Let's refrain from any suggestions of demolition or renovation," Monty said, heading for the door. "I want no inference pointing to any involvement on our part for any destruction suffered by this edifice."

"Just suggesting that the Tate Treatment would actually *help* this place out," I said, following him. "It can only go up in aesthetics and property value. We can let Peaches add a canine touch to the place. Totally new meaning for dog house."

"Clever," Monty said, glancing at Peaches. "Not clever enough to condone the wholesale destruction of this building. Grey may own the Abyss, but there are interested parties involved, powerful interested parties, who would take violent offense at its destruction."

"Doesn't have to be wholesale destruction, we can make it

retail and scale it down to minor destruction," I said. "Just the facade."

"Let's not," Monty said, looking across the street at the van sitting there and waiting for us. "Activate the defenses on our vehicle."

I placed a hand on the Dark Goat's surface.

A wave of orange energy ran along the entire chassis, causing runic symbols to appear as the energy spread out along the body of the vehicle.

The sound of a hammer on an anvil clanged into the early evening as the Dark Goat locked down. For a split second I almost wished the magistrate would try to do something to my car, but I quickly shut that thought down as I recalled the melting of the original Goat.

"I hope Cecil beefed up the defenses on the Dark Goat," I said. "I want to go on the record right now and say that I will not be responsible for my actions if Emeric melts the Dark Goat."

"Cecil is exceptional when it comes to our vehicles, and they managed to withstand the punishment we dole out," Monty said, glancing at the Dark Goat and running a hand along its body. "He may want the means to undo this vehicle, but I think, deep down, he's proud of its indestructibility."

I patted the hood and nodded as I glared across the street, giving the black van my best death stare.

"We should go over there and melt them first," I said, still keeping my eyes on the van. "They can't attack us if they are recovering in Haven from multiple injuries."

"We don't want the Emissary here, at least not yet," Monty said. "An unprovoked attack will only escalate matters. Let's go see Grey and LD."

At the rear of the building we located the nondescript service entrance. Monty stepped close to what appeared to be a plain industrial door and gestured, letting white symbols float from his fingers to the surface.

It unlocked with a click.

Monty pulled on the door and we entered the museum.

We stayed in the service area, following a flight of stairs down to the lowest level. As hard as I tried, I couldn't make out the entrance to the Abyss proper.

I examined the wall and came back with nothing. Not even trying to look for it with my innersight worked. Whatever obfuscation runes had been used were stronger than my sight.

The last time we had been here, Albert was with us. I didn't bring it up because that family reunion, hadn't ended well...for Albert.

Or Monty actually.

It was the one time he had taken on the mantle of the Harbinger.

I don't know if Dex let him wear the mantle because he was getting Monty ready to take his place eventually, or because he couldn't face Albert as the Harbinger, knowing what he would have to do.

Dex had spared Albert once; it was possible he didn't trust himself not to let him go again. By letting Monty wear the mantle of the Harbinger—justice—the justice Albert had evaded for so long, was carried out.

Did I believe it was justice?

I honestly didn't know.

What I did know was that it was a Montague family issue, and my last name was clearly *not* Montague, which meant I was going to keep out of it as long as Monty didn't start turning into some version of the Harbinger against his will.

"Can you sense the runes?" Monty asked. "Grey seems to have altered them."

"He boosted your runes?" I asked looking at the space where I remembered the entrance was situated. "Can he do that to your runes?"

"He *is* strong enough," Monty said with a nod. "It's not exactly boosting. Their power level hasn't changed; he modified them slightly. Made them more sensitive and"—he ran a hand along the wall—"it appears he added some additional layers of lethality."

"Of course he did," I said, moving back from the wall cautiously. "Because what does every defensive setup call for? More layers of lethality."

"In this case you would be right," Monty said. "The Abyss is recognized as an official meeting place for dark mages. Extra layers of lethality in its defenses is prudent, and expected."

Monty stepped forward and placed a hand on the wall.

The wall shimmered for a few seconds, then disappeared revealing a staircase leading down. This staircase was unlike the one in the Whitney. This was a staircase of instant pain if you made a wrong move.

Rows of runes covered every step as we descended. Every step gave off a soft orange glow. Normally, that would be inviting, but I could make out some of these runes and they all meant the same thing: if you're not invited and you made it this far, enjoy the view because it's the last thing you're going to see.

We reached the last step and faced a heavily runed steel door.

It was more of a runed steel slab set into the wall.

There was no obvious locking mechanism or handle. As far as anyone was concerned, there was no way to get past this door.

Another level of defense.

Monty looked up at the small camera situated above the

door and pointing down at us. I remembered that beneath our feet was a series of oblivion circles that could be activated if anyone tried to breach the Abyss this way.

That attempt would end in a bloody and short-lived failure.

Peaches sniffed the air and rumbled.

<*Frank is close. It will be good to see him again.*>

<*He is? That's good. Frank and I need to have a conversation about some of the information he's been feeding you.*>

<*Feeding? I'm starving. Can I have some meat once we go inside?*>

<*I'll see what I can do; you just ate a little while ago.*>

<*It was too long ago. Before that you tried to feed me your healthy meat which hurt my stomach. That was bad.*>

<*Not as bad as the slobber-mangling you kept giving me. You could have taken it easy. I'm your bondmate after all.*>

<*As your bondmate, I want you to be your strongest. You should eat more meat.*>

<*I eat plenty of meat. Excuse me if I'm not on the hellhound level of meat devouring. I have a normal stomach.*>

<*If you were eating more meat, you would be much stronger. We could use our battleform and no one could stop us.*>

It was a mildly scary thought and from what I understood, mostly true. It was one of the reasons we had been targeted for elimination before we stepped fully into our power.

I patted him on the head and rubbed behind his ears as he rumbled at me.

<*Some of us can't manage eating an entire cow in one sitting. I'll stick to the average amount of meat method, thanks. You still smell Frank?*>

<*Yes. Don't forget to call him a dragon. He likes it when people call him a dragon.*>

<*A dragon I can squish with one boot isn't much of a dragon, you*

know. He's a lizard. One with an overinflated sense of importance, but still a lizard. Why do you entertain his delusion of being a dragon?>

<He sees himself as a dragon and he is my friend. He likes to be called a dragon. We do things for our friends, even if we don't always understand them. Don't you do things for your friends?>

<I do, but I'm not going to call that liz...>

Right then, he hit me with a maximum dose of puppy dog eyes that caught me totally off-guard.

<What are you doing? Cut that out.>

<I'm using my hellhound charm. Frank says that it can be very effective, especially when I don't want to bite someone or if I want extra food. He says it makes me unrestrictable.>

<I think you mean irresistible, and it doesn't. Stop it.>

I tried my best to keep my gaze averted and failed.

He moved around and nudged my leg with his head as he let out a low growl followed by a rumble and a whine.

"What is wrong with your creature?" Monty asked, looking down at Peaches. "Is he hungry—again?"

"No, we are discussing how a certain lizard should be addressed," I said. "He says dragon, I'm opting for roadkill."

"Frank is very close to Grey," Monty said, giving me a look. "In addition, I have it on good authority that while his transmutation failed, causing him to inhabit the body of a thorny dragon, he still retains *all* his mage abilities, which are formidable."

"In the body of a lizard."

"Splitting an atom releases an astronomical amount of energy," Monty said. "What does it matter that he is in the body of a lizard? Technically he is correct, the body he inhabits is that of a thorny *dragon*. You lose nothing by addressing him as such."

"It's not the whole dragon thing that irks me," I said,

waving his words away. "It's the ideas he tries to put in my hellhound's head. He's looking for a good squashing."

Monty shook his head.

"Aside from the improbability of an attempted squashing, threatening or attempting to threaten him would cause animosity between you, and both Frank and Grey. That would be unwise and foolhardy."

He had a point and I didn't need an angry Grey pointing his sword at me. Grey was older, more cunning, and stronger than Monty. If I had to classify his power level, I would place him close to Dex and that was a scary thought.

The sword he wielded, which was the pair to Ebonsoul, was sentient, with the mind of a bloodthirsty goddess, which if the theories were correct, was the actual first vampire to exist.

Getting on Grey's bad side wouldn't be a smart move.

"Agreed," I said. "I'll be civil and maybe call him a *dragon*."

Monty nodded before looking up at the camera.

"Banshee, Deathless, and Sausage," he said, staring at the camera. "TK will be here shortly and we have some unwanted stragglers across the street."

"Deathless?" I said. "Is that my Abyss code name? Do I get a decoder ring too? Maybe a special ID?"

"I didn't create it," he said with a sigh. "If you dislike it, take it up with Grey."

"Sausage?" I said glancing at my hellhound. "Really?"

"I actually think that one is quite apt," Monty said. "If he keeps on his current dietary trajectory, he will resemble one soon enough."

I did have to agree with Monty on this one.

A few seconds later, the door slid to the side, revealing a darkened lounge area I recalled from my last visit here. Jonathan Roy could be heard over the speakers in the background. His husky voice filled the space as he shared about the fire keeping him alive. I enjoyed the music for a few beats as the heavily runed door sealed behind us.

The aroma of rich, dark, and strong Death Wish javambrosia filled my lungs, surrounding me as I closed my eyes, took a deep breath, and sighed.

If heaven had a smell, it was this, exactly this.

FOURTEEN

Grey might be a bad-tempered dark mage, bonded to a bloodthirsty goddess and friends to a lizard with delusions of grandeur, but he had excellent taste in music and coffee. He had also saved my and Monty's lives on more than one occasion and that meant he was family in my book.

Insane family, but still family. There were never any guarantees of sanity or normalcy with found family. You took what you found or, in my case, what found you.

I looked around the dimly lit space.

Opposite the door was a long bar.

I looked around for the lizard but didn't see him.

I didn't even sense him, which meant that even though my hellhound stated that Frank was here, there was a good chance we just missed him.

Behind the bar, wearing a casual dress shirt and jeans, stood Grey Stryder working on making some coffee. His ever-present duster hung on a coat rack a few feet away. From what my senses told me, he was the only one in the Abyss.

"One sec," he said, without turning and holding up a

finger. "This is almost done and if I don't have this now, the world will be unsafe."

"You drinking coffee makes the world safe?"

"If I drink coffee, I'm less irritable," he said. "My being less irritable makes the world a safer place, trust me."

"What happens if you *don't* drink this coffee?" I asked. "Inquiring minds want to know."

He glanced back at me with a scowl.

"The headache, which is currently crushing my skull and slowly working its way down my spine, is going to make me unpleasant company," he said, turning back to the coffee he was making. "If it doesn't kill me first."

"Not fun," I said. "That sounds like a painful way to die."

"If it doesn't kill me, which is unlikely due to my blade, I will be cranky and in a foul mood for the foreseeable future. Amazingly, no one likes me in a foul mood, imagine that," he continued. "Without my coffee, I will be irritable and less than my usual jovial welcoming self. So, if you don't mind, give me a few seconds?"

"Please," Monty said. "Don't let us stop you. Drink as much as you need."

"Strong?" Grey said over his shoulder without turning. "Need a cup? This is a little stronger than you may be used to. Think you can handle it?"

"I'll take a mug, thanks."

"A mug?" he said, laughed, and then turned to give me a look. "Oh, you're serious. No, I don't think so, don't need your heart exploding while you're here. It's messy and unnecessary. You get the *demitasse*. Anything for you, Tea and Crumpets?"

"The usual please," Monty said. "Thank you."

"Earl Grey, well steeped," Grey said, shaking his head. "Never could get used to your leafy water."

"Demitasse?" I asked. "That's barely enough to get started."

"You'll thank me later, trust me," Grey said. "No need to test the limits of your curse."

I raised my hand in surrender and let him pour the coffee as I continued to look around.

"Where's Frank?"

"You just missed him," Grey said with some concern in his voice. "As my head of security, he needed to take care of some of the defensive runes over at The Dive. Why?"

"No reason," I said, glancing at my hellhound. "Peaches wanted to see his friend, the *dragon*."

Grey gave me a look and raised an eyebrow in a familiar mage-like way, reminding me of a curious Spock right before he found something fascinating.

"I sense you have an issue with him being called a dragon," he said, placing his mug on the bar. "Why?"

"Because he's a lizard?" I said. "He is *not* a dragon. Not by any stretch of the imagination."

"*Moloch horridus*—mountain devil, thorny lizard, and thorny *dragon*," Grey explained. "He is technically correct. He *is* a dragon, just not a very large one."

"*Moloch* is a species of lizard," I explained. If he could flex his knowledge, so could I. "I've faced dragons, real dragons, trying to stomp me out of existence on more than one occasion. Frank is not a dragon, not even close."

"I'm sensing some pent-up hostility," Grey said, staring at me. "Why don't we address this?"

"Let's," I said. "To start, Frank has no business calling himself a dragon."

"Simon..." Monty said. "I strongly advise against—"

"I've had my coffee, Tea and Crumpets," Grey said, holding up a hand in Monty's direction. "I promise not to blast him, at least nowhere that will do lasting damage." He turned to me. "Go on. You were saying, Frank is not a dragon."

"I don't know why he insists on calling himself one," I continued against my better judgement. "Especially to Peaches."

"So it's not the calling himself a dragon, per se," Grey said. "It's that he calls himself a dragon to your hound?"

"Yes, he's misrepresenting himself and Peaches believes him."

"I see, and you're here to represent the Authentic Dragons Image Union?" Grey asked, facing me fully. "You're here to take offense for all *true* dragons, that Frank chooses to call himself a dragon, while actually being a lizard, is that it?"

"It's not that, it's—"

"When did they nominate you as their representative?" he asked with a dangerous smile. "Which I find odd, since every encounter *I've* had with a dragon, they were decidedly intent on ending me. Sounds a little counterintuitive to make you their representative, if you ask me."

"They didn't nominate me for anything," I said. "It's just I don't think—"

I saw Monty shake his head out of the corner of my eye.

"You don't approve of the advice he gives your hellhound?"

"Not particularly, no."

"Ah," Grey said with a nod. "Now we're getting somewhere. Has he turned your hound against you? Made him your enemy?"

"Well, no."

"Has Frank portrayed you in a negative light to your hellhound or to anyone else?"

"No."

"Has he tried to break the bond between you and your bondmate?" Grey asked. "You know, has he told your hound to abandon you, leave you to roam the planes, that sort of thing?"

"He hasn't. That's a thing?" I asked. "Hellhounds can just leave?"

"Not usually with the bonded, but they can and have, when unbonded," Grey said as he leaned back against the bar. "It never ends well, for anyone. Now that I think of it, how many friends *does* your hound have?"

"To my knowledge, Peaches has an entire little group of friends with Frank, Cece, Peanut and Rags."

"Ah, got it," Grey said with a nod and slid a tiny cup filled with black coffee in front of me. "Frank did mention this. They have a whole little group thing going on from what I understand. The Brew and Chew Crew. Cute."

"Yes, cute."

"Is it possible, just maybe, you're taking issue with an entirely different aspect here," Grey added. "I mean, besides, that whole incident where they had to *rescue* you?"

"It wasn't a rescue."

"Are you feeling left out?" Grey asked. "I'm sure I can put in a good word with Frank and get you included in the Brew and Chew Crew, if they're taking on new members that is. I know how important it can be to feel included.

"I don't want to join their crew."

"You sure? Though I don't really know who the leader of the group is," he continued. "Maybe you can ask your hound. I'm sure he can get you in. Maybe honorary status?"

"I don't want to get 'in' and, for the record, they didn't *rescue* me."

"Sure they didn't," Grey said with a small smile before taking a sip of coffee from his mug. "Since it seems you may be misinformed, let clarify this a bit for you. Just to assist your understanding."

"That would be excellent. Please do."

Grey nodded and took another sip from his mug, before placing it down on the bar next to him. He cleared his throat and like every mage I knew, entered full-blown professor explainer mode.

"We all know names have power, we understand it, and we live it. Can we agree on that?"

Monty nodded.

"This is a basic tenet for mages," Monty said. "Names can correlate directly to the power of an item or being."

"Sure," I said. "Names define and can impart attributes."

"Well said," Grey said, raising his mug in my direction. "How many names do you have now, Strong?"

"What does that have to do with anything?"

"How many?" he pressed. "I'm curious."

"Simon Strong," I said with finality. "How many names do I need?"

"In the world of magic you currently inhabit, quite a few, it seems," he said, counting on his fingers. "The Cursed and Marked of Kali, Aspis to Mage Montague, Bondmate to the scion of Cerberus, Wielder of a Necrotic Seraph, that's four so far, am I missing any?"

"Stormblood bound," Monty volunteered and shrugged when I gave him an extra dose of stink-eye. "He did ask."

"So five, so far," Grey said. "I'm sure I'm missing one or more, like Most Aggravating Immortal, or Bearer of the Suicidal Wit."

"Night Warden humor is almost as bad as mage humor, but worse," I said. "What are you trying to say?"

"That you currently have six names, including Simon Strong."

"Those others aren't names," I countered. "They're titles, and I didn't give any of those to myself. They were placed upon me. Usually against my will."

"Does that matter?" Grey asked. "That fact is irrelevant.

In this world of magic you inhabit, there are beings who don't know who Simon Strong is, but mention the Marked of Kali, or the Aspis, and all of a sudden they know and hate you with a passion."

I nodded.

"That's been made clear more than once."

"Those *titles* are more identifying than your actual name," Grey said. "They help form your identity, shaping how people interact and relate to you. Do you agree?"

"Yes," I said, hesitatingly. "Although, the shape is usually a blade, an orb, or some other weapon, while the relating and interacting is usually homicidal in nature."

"Comes with the titles; it's no picnic being a Night Warden, either," he said. "I've never won any popularity contests. Everything seems like it wants to retire me violently. Doesn't change who or what I am—I'm still a Night Warden."

"I'm not seeing what this has to—"

"Frank is a dragon, a friend, and *my family*," Grey said his words laced with an undercurrent of steel. "I know you understand the concept of family."

"I do."

"From what I understand, you seem to be extremely protective of those you consider to be part of yours."

I nodded and began to think that bringing up this topic may have been a mistake. Grey was probably as protective of his family as I was of mine.

"I am."

Grey gave me a slow nod, paused, and took another sip.

"Frank is a dragon, not because he resides in the body of a dragon, but because he has a heart fiercer than any dragon you have, or ever will, face," he said. "He has chosen to present himself as a dragon and you will do him the courtesy of addressing him as such, *or* he will unleash enough power on your person to test your curse several times over, be well within his rights to do so, and all I will do is sweep up what's left of you when he does."

"As long as he stops trying to corrupt my hellhound, " I said, not ready to back down so easily. "I'll call him whatever he wants."

Grey laughed and set me at ease.

"You've already lost *that* battle, Strong," he said. "Accept it and move on. They're friends, as hard as that is to believe, and, if you ever need anyone at your back when things go dark, you can do worse than Frank. He may be small, but he packs quite a punch."

"It's possible that we just need to have a conversation," I said, taking the small cup of coffee in one hand and reconsidering my attitude toward the liz-dragon. "Frank and I have never really had a chance to connect."

"Probably not the best of ideas," Grey said, shaking his head. "Frank is actually more on the anti-social side. He keeps his circle close and small, for the safety of all involved. Speaking of, I did miss *one* of your names, the latest one."

"Which?" I asked. "You went through all of the titles."

"You have a new one, recently acquired," Grey answered. "Outcast."

FIFTEEN

"True," Monty said. "The Grand Council has seen to that."

Grey nodded and motioned to the tiny cup in my hand.

"Best if you drink it hot," he said, giving me a wary look. "Try to pace yourself."

I looked down at the tiny cup in my hand.

"Pace myself?" I asked. "What is this, three ounces of coffee and you want me to pace myself? Seriously?"

"Seriously," he said, making a sipping motion with his hand, even holding out his pinky finger. "Small sips are your friend."

"You do realize I drink—"

"Nothing even remotely close in potency to what is in that cup," Grey finished. "Trust me, this is a special brew for *my* headaches. You don't want or need more than what's in there. Not if you want to sleep this month."

I smiled at his attempt to impress me with the strength of his coffee. There was no way it could be stronger than what I was used to. I was certain my Death Wish javambrosia was much stronger than what I held in my hand.

I was wrong.

I didn't chug it down, I took a small sip, just in case he wasn't exaggerating, and put the cup down. The effect was nearly immediate. I don't know how he brewed this particular version of Death Wish, but if I hadn't been cursed alive, I'd seriously question my ability to survive this coffee.

It was strong…too strong.

My heart immediately went into EDM overdrive, ramping up to what felt like five-hundred beats per minute, all the colors of the spectrum and some I was certain didn't belong, suddenly came into high definition, accompanied with a hybrid epic soundtrack composed by Hans Zimmer and John Williams trying to explode my brain as it drowned out all sound in my ears.

The entire Abyss exploded with slowly swaying runic symbols glowing different shades of orange, violet, blue and green. A bass undercurrent vibrated in my abdomen, filling my ears. I could swear a group of French horns were hidden somewhere, playing one long note behind the bar to add an ominous ambiance to the space.

"What in the actual hell?" I said as I staggered in front of the bar, before gripping the side to prevent myself from stumbling. "That's not normal Death Wish."

"I did say you needed to pace yourself," he said, pointing to my cup. "That's a special blend."

"That's a special, lethal blend."

"It can be," he said, taking a large sausage from the fridge behind the bar, placing it in a large titanium bowl, and sliding it toward my hellhound. "I'm sure your hound is hungry."

Peaches advanced on the sausage and gave me a look. I nodded and he proceeded to devour the meat.

"Guess he *was* hungry," Grey continued, then glanced at me. "That coffee is very much like the situation you two currently find yourselves in. Although Tea and Crumpets here doesn't partake, the metaphor still applies."

He nodded at Monty who nodded back and sipped his tea.

"What do you mean?"

Grey took a long pull from his mug before placing it on the bar.

"This blend of coffee is the situation you two now find yourselves in," he said, pointing to the mug. "You're used to your regular Death Wish, like you're finally used to this world of magic. This current situation is like my special blend, unknown, extremely powerful, and lethal."

"Really? We're doing Zen coffee lessons now?"

He took another pull from his mug before continuing.

"Keeping it simple so you can comprehend the level of hate you're facing," he said. "The Grand Council put the word out on you two. Magus non grata—everywhere."

"But I'm not—"

He raised his hand and shook his head.

"Before you start with the, 'I'm not a mage' line of denial, don't bother," he said. "You cast a magic missile, are bonded to a hellhound, and manipulate energy with that bubble of yours—dawnrise, or whatever you call it."

"Dawnward."

"Yes, that," he continued. "Then there's the matter of your attack."

"What attack?"

"You attempted to attack a magistrate in the official capacity of delivering an edict, not exactly one of your brighter moves there," he explained. "That makes you mage *enough* to get exterminated along with Tea and Crumpets here, according to the GC."

"Magus non grata," Monty said pensive. "Everywhere? They've broadcast the status?"

"Everywhere it matters," Grey said. "All the neutral zones are to refuse you services: Hellfire Club, Hybrid, Dark Council, Light Council, and any council in between. Even the NYTF has been notified about your new status."

"What about the other sects?" I asked. "Them too?"

"Them *especially*," Grey said. "The other sects, High Tribunal, and of course, Verity, goes without saying. No one is your friend right now, at least not overtly."

"How come the Night Wardens weren't warned to stay away from us?" I asked. "Does the Grand Council not consider you under its jurisdiction?"

"Who says we weren't?" Grey answered. "They advised us to limit any interaction with you, Tea and Crumpets here, and Dex."

"Then, I'm curious, why are we here?"

"Night Wardens have never taken instructions outside of our organization well," Grey said. "We don't technically fall under the Grand Council's jurisdiction. We're not a sect nor one of the Councils."

"What exactly are the Night Wardens?"

"The ones you call when all hope is lost," Grey said. "We're the ones who will be there at the end. When everyone else has fallen, you better believe a Night Warden will be standing beside you."

"The Grand Council can't force the Night Wardens?"

"All they can do is strongly advise," Grey answered. "But they can't enforce the edict with the Night Wardens."

"There are still some who will stand with us," Monty said. "The Ten, the Midnight Echelon, and even Division 13."

"Scratch Division 13 off that list," Grey said, shaking his head. "Ronin and the entire Division are shady. They only stand with Division 13 and you two don't qualify."

"We don't?" I asked, wondering who was in Division 13. "Really?"

"Really, you don't, and frankly, I'm surprised you've even heard of them."

"Midnight Echelon will back us up," I said.

"Very likely, since Midnight Echelon is as fringe as it gets and mentally questionable. They do love a good fight, though, so no surprise there. You mentioned the Ten?"

"The Ten always has our back."

"Nothing really to brag about there," Grey said with a slight shrug. "That's like being friends with Dex. He has tremendous clout and power off-the-charts, but people are either scared of him or hate him. That hatred, mixed with unreasonable fear will carry over to you two. It's not quite the benefit you may think it is."

"What about Sebastian?" I asked, glancing at Monty. "Monty's cousin?"

"The Stray Dogs are interesting," Grey said, tapping his chin. "They move in very different circles, outside your usual orbit. The Grand Council has no direct influence in the magical Underworld."

"But?" I said. "I'm sensing a 'but' there."

"No *direct* influence, but since it's the *magical* Underworld, the Grand Council can and does act, let's say *indirectly*, to achieve their goals."

"What does that mean?" I asked. "Indirectly?"

"It means, they will be ten times as ruthless when moving in that world," Monty said. "They have no need for edicts, rules, or regulations to hinder or hamper them from acting exactly as they want to act."

"Ten times worse?"

Grey nodded.

"It's not good to broadcast your affiliation with the Stray Dogs," Grey said. "You will attract some nasty characters you'd prefer you didn't, but Treadwell can be helpful in a pinch. I wouldn't want to tangle with that Tiger, she's dangerous."

"So we're down to the Ten and a Night Warden?" I asked. "Against the entire Grand Council?"

"You say that like it's a bad thing," Grey said, feigning offense. "The Night Wardens may not have the numbers, and the Ten, well there's at *least* ten of them, if not more. I think the odds are about even if you ask me."

"I count thirteen against the entire Grand Council and you're saying the odds are about even?" I asked, incredulous. "How many mages do the Grand Council have?"

"At least a few thousand, if not more," Grey said, making my heart sink at the thought that we ever had a chance. "Don't forget they are truly a worldwide organization. There's no escaping them."

I stared at him.

"Just how strong are you making that coffee?" I asked. "Because right now, you're sounding delusional. How can you say the odds are about even? We're seriously outnumbered and outgunned."

"Outnumbered, yes. Outgunned? I don't think so," he said. "You have never seen the Ten when they're serious. I almost feel sorry for the Grand Council. By the way, did you include your hound in the count?"

"No," I said. "Fine, fourteen, against how many? Hundreds, Thousands?"

"Probably in the tens if not the hundreds of thousands."

"How is that remotely even?"

"You're still not getting it," Grey said after taking another pull from his mug. "This is not a numbers game. This is a powers game."

"I don't understand," I said. "They have the numbers and the power."

"They have the numbers," Grey said, "but their power is concentrated in the upper echelons of their organizational structure."

"How many are in this structure?" I asked. "What kind of numbers?"

"The Grand Council itself, which is a group of five fairly powerful mages, the five Emissaries, who serve them, and the five magistrates who serve the Emissaries."

"Fifteen sounds doable."

"Well, they do have thousands of Sanitizers, venomancers, and many other kinds of magic users," he said. "It's not a cakewalk either. Our goal is to stop the magistrate assigned to erase you and bloody the Emissary before he gets any bright ideas."

Monty nodded.

"That should dissuade them from pursuing this further," Monty said. "If we make an example of the magistrate and the Emissary, it should convince the Grand Council that we are more trouble than we're worth."

"That's one strategy," Grey said. "Or you can go scorched earth and remove everyone from the upper echelons except the actual Grand Council."

"Won't that start this all over again?" I asked. "They'll just send another magistrate and armies of Sanitizers."

"I hate to burst your little bubble of self-importance," Grey said. "But despite the fact that they issued this edict, you're not that important to them. Now, Dex, that's a different matter entirely. For him, they might go to war."

"Because of the Golden Circle?"

"Because he dared to stand against them."

SIXTEEN

"Dex isn't really a fan of authority, *any* kind of authority."

"He stole a sect," Grey said. "I don't know what possessed the old man to do that, but for the Grand Council, it's the principle. They're not exactly fans of Dexter, and this could be the straw that shatters the camel's back."

"Which means we have to drive our point home with certainty, leaving no room for them to misconstrue our intentions," Monty said. "We have to convince the Emissary and the Grand Council that this is a battle they do not want."

"The Grand Council doesn't like to get their hands dirty," Grey said. "That works in your favor. The large amounts of Sanitizers they're willing to throw at you because of what's at stake does not."

"TK said that LD would meet us here," I said. "Do you know if he's on his way?"

"I heard the same thing," Grey said. "But if TK said he'll meet you here, he will meet you here. I haven't seen him yet, but there's a good chance he's just getting ready."

"Getting ready?" I asked. "Getting ready for what?"

A tremor rumbled through the Abyss.

"That," Grey said. "I think the magistrate is done waiting."

"He's attacking us?" I asked, incredulous. "I thought the Abyss was a neutral zone?"

"Not exactly," Grey said, grabbing his duster from the nearby coat-hook. "It's a meeting place for dark mages, but it's no neutral zone. They were most likely waiting for authorization from the Emissary to launch their attack."

I looked around at the interior of the Abyss.

It was an upscale version of The Dive—a *very* upscale version. Everything gave off an aura of luxury, from the polished wood floor to the chaises situated around the edges of the room. Even the bar, which I was certain was Australian Buloke, was stained a deep brown and subtly covered in intricate runes.

"Looks like they got it," I said, glancing at the door. "You think LD is out there on his own?"

He looked up at a screen that showed several external views.

"Not for long," Grey said. "I can't let them unload on the Abyss and more importantly, you don't let people attack Night Wardens."

"Even if it's the Grand Council?"

"Doesn't matter who they are," Grey said, taking one last sip of coffee. "If they aren't met with some kind of response, it sets a bad precedent. Next thing you know, everyone is lining up to blow Night Wardens to bits. That is unacceptable. There may not be many of us—"

"Two, last time I checked," I said. "There are only two of you."

"Correct," Grey said, giving me a look. "But you only need one of us to turn the tide of any battle. Trust me, you wouldn't want Koda here; she's still a little young and takes attacks like these personally. It never ends well for the attacker."

"Need to work on her tact."

"Sure," Grey said with a nod. "This, from the trio that has single-handedly renovated entire parts of this city. Entire neighborhoods have been rebuilt because of your fights."

"Extenuating circumstances," I said. "Not our fault at all."

I heard Monty cough behind me.

"For someone who's quick to claim they aren't a mage, you sure sound like one," Grey said. "When we get outside, let me do the talking until it's no longer time to talk."

"You're going to cast?" Monty asked concerned. "That wouldn't be wise."

"Not unless I have to," Grey answered adjusting his duster. "I'm not looking forward to a worse headache, since Simon is already here."

"Oh, haha, Warden humor," I deadpanned. "Hilarious really."

"I know, now move aside."

I stepped to one side and gave Grey space near the edge of the bar.

Grey placed his hand on one side of the bar as we headed to the door. I looked behind us and saw a nightmare of oblivion circles activate as he crossed the floor to the exit.

Once we were at the door, he pressed his hand on a section of the door and all of the defenses that I could see became active.

"I don't think anyone would make it past the front door, but if they ever did, they won't survive what's waiting for them in there."

"That's the point," Grey said, still holding his mug of coffee. "Let's go see who wants to stop breathing today."

We headed upstairs and onto the street.

When we exited the Abyss, we stood on an elevated

section of an abandoned railway that had been converted into a linear park.

"The rear of the Abyss leads to the High Line?" I asked looking around. "Since when?"

"It doesn't," Grey said. "The rear of the Whitney Museum leads to the High Line Park. Remember, The Abyss doesn't exist to the normal public."

He stepped ahead and looked down at the corner of Washington and Gansevoort Streets. What I used to remember as the Meat Packing District was now a tourist attraction with a strolling park in the center of it.

Monty and I joined him at the edge of the High Line and looked down. Across the street near the van stood Emeric and a group of mages.

I couldn't make out how many since they were currently clown vanning their vehicle. Every few seconds a new Sanitizer—or what I assumed was a Sanitizer—would drop out of the van.

"They have some sort of portal in that thing?" I asked. "There's no way they all fit inside that van."

"Similar principle to the pockets in my duster," Grey said, still scanning the street. "Not as elegant, but useful. No need to drive around in a convoy when you have a pocket dimension."

"There are at least twenty of them down there without the magistrate," I said, gazing down at the Grand Council minions. "I don't see LD."

"Right here, hombre," a voice said next to me and nearly startled my heart into leaping out of my chest. "I'm just giving them a moment to gather themselves."

"What the—?" I said, raising my voice and whirling on LD. "You didn't think letting us know you were there was a good idea?"

LD chuckled.

"*They* knew I was here," he said, pointing at Grey and Monty. "I'm pretty sure even Peaches knew I was sitting right here. Take a deep breath, Strong." He gave Grey a look. "Have you been giving him your coffee?"

"Small cup," Grey said. "He may be a little high-strung until it works its way out of his system."

LD shook his head.

"Never drink Night Warden coffee," he said, gesturing. "I made that mistake once."

LD materialized a large sausage and proceeded to feed it to my ever-voracious hellhound. Peaches gently removed the sausage from his fingers and then instantly hoovered it from sight.

"Good boy," LD said, looking across the street and pointing with his chin. "The magistrate is in the back near the van."

"Most likely positioning himself for a quick exit if need be," Monty said. "They're using an interdimensional portal, from inside the van. It's generating a substantial energy signature and drawing on a power source located in the front of the van. Three mages are currently powering it."

"What did they use on the building?" Grey asked, looking up at the Whitney. "Any external damage?"

"Concussive blast, with a disintegration component," LD answered. "I covered the building. You may have felt a tremor, but no actual damage. I think they're getting ready to use big guns. I was about to go inside when they started, so I figured I'd wait for you all out here."

"How did you know we'd end up out here?"

"I didn't, but I know Grey," LD said with a grin. "He doesn't like his building being attacked. Night Wardens have a rep to maintain."

"We do," Grey said, then took a pull from his mug, which

I was beginning to think was as bottomless as his duster pockets. "How do you want to play this?"

"Your base, your play," LD said. "I'm here to make sure they don't grab these three. The magistrate is the real threat; the minions might be a problem because of their numbers."

"We need to disable the portal," Monty said. "That will diminish the numbers advantage."

"We'll try diplomacy," Grey said. "Violence doesn't always have to be the default response."

"Hasn't been my experience, but sure, knock yourself out," I said. "Go talk some sense into them. Magistrate's name is Emeric by the way, works for Emissary Dubois."

"Dubois?" Grey said. "The Bloody Scythe?"

"You know him?"

"I know *of* him," Grey put his mug down on a bench. "Shit, this is going to get messy. Dubois is an aggressive, arrogant, narrow-minded mage who believes his own press."

"Sounds like a few mages I know."

"True," Grey said. "Except Dubois has the power to back up his delusions of grandeur. It hasn't helped that the Grand Council elevated him in position. Damn it."

"All yours," LD said. "If I were you,"—he looked at his watch—"whatever you're going to do, you want to do it before TK gets here. She unleashed an unkindness earlier, so you can imagine what kind of mood she's in."

"Homicidal, and that's putting it nicely," Grey said. "Fine, let's get this resolved before she gets here and everything dies."

"Good plan," LD said, motioning to the edge of the High Line. "After you. You three, hold here, in case they get creative and try a rear attack."

Grey picked up his mug, stepped to the edge and jumped over the railing of the High Line, then floated down to the street level. LD did the same, but remained directly below us.

SEVENTEEN

"Grey Stryder," Emeric said, pronouncing the name with contempt as his Sanitizers fanned out to either side of the street. "The last Night Warden. To what do I owe this honor?"

Grey stepped forward into the semicircle of death.

"The honor is mine," Grey said, his voice carrying clearly across the street. "Meeting a magistrate working for Alain is quite rare. Is he going to join us this evening?"

Emeric's features twisted at the mention of the emissary's name without the honorific. I could see Grey smile at the reaction.

"*Emissary* Dubois, is busy with more important affairs, as befits his station," Emeric said emphasizing the title. "He has entrusted me with the resolution of this matter."

"What exactly *is* the matter that brings you to my neighborhood?"

Emeric looked up to where Monty and I stood and then returned his gaze to Grey.

"By order of the Grand Council, Tristan Montague and Simon Strong, along with his canine of questionable origin, are to be erased and eliminated," Emeric said. "Should any third party interfere, it will be considered an act of aggression, not only against my person as a representative of the Emissary, but against the entire Grand Council."

Grey remained silent and took a long pull from his mug, never taking his eyes off Emeric. A few of the Sanitizers fanned out farther, trying to encircle Grey.

Grey turned slowly and gazed up at us for a few seconds before turning back to Emeric and his Sanitizers.

"The Grand Council?" he said. "That's some major attention. Aside from some minor property damage, I don't recall these three requiring corrective action from such an esteemed body. What changed?"

Emeric stepped forward a few steps as some of his Sanitizers made space for him in the semicircle. He glared at Grey as he did so.

"What changed?" he asked. "More like what *hasn't* changed—Dexter Montague. He is the reason they will be erased and eliminated. He, too faces the same edict."

"Serious consequences," Grey said after a few moments. "What did *he* do?"

"That does not concern you, Night Warden," Emeric scoffed, using Grey's title and waving his words away. "You only need to hand them over; we will be on our way and you... you can continue with whatever it is Night Wardens do with their meaningless existence."

Below us, LD shook his head and said some words under his breath.

"...this magistrate is suicidal," I managed to catch as LD began to step forward. "Grey..."

Grey held up a hand without turning around.

"I'm good," Grey said. "Been drinking my coffee all day."

I saw Grey move his duster aside and create access to his gun, Fatebringer. I always thought Grim Whisper was dangerous, but I had seen Grey's gun up close and in action. It wasn't a weapon I ever wanted to face.

Still, I'd rather face that gun than his sword, Darkspirit. If Grey drew his blade, all of the Grand Council minions in front of him were dead.

It was why LD was concerned. Even though Grey came across as cranky and irritable—and he was—most of the time, he was calm and laid back.

It didn't mean he wasn't dangerous.

Grey was also a dark mage bonded to a powerful bloodthirsty goddess. Emphasis on the bloodthirsty. The goddess, Izanami, constantly tried to tempt Grey into giving her complete control of his body.

For Grey, I imagined it was a constant battle to keep her confined to the blade he was bonded to. The arrangement he had entered into with her took Faustian bargains to a nightmarish level.

Grey was dying.

It was a situation he had made peace with. He was prepared to leave on his own terms when Hades had given him Darkspirit.

By bonding to the blade, Izanami extended his life, keeping him alive, but locking him into their agreement. I couldn't prove it, but deep inside, I knew this was another of Hades' shadow moves.

She needed a vessel, a body that wasn't a blade, and Grey was the perfect vessel, a powerful, ancient dark mage.

What she didn't count on was Grey being a Night Warden and believing in their principles. He may have been a dark mage, but there was no way she was going to corrupt him to turn against his beliefs.

If she ever took over and got control of Grey, the Grand Council was the least of our worries.

We'd need all of the Ten and probably Dex to slow him

down. That was a fight I never wanted to see, much less be a part of.

It was why Grey drank his special blend of coffee and why he stuck to Night Warden affairs. I think if Grey had his way, he would've retired from the Night Wardens long ago.

His sense of duty, and the fact that he was training Koda as the next Night Warden, prevented him from leaving the streets he protected with his life.

To call his existence meaningless was not only suicidal, but a major insult. To Grey, the Night Wardens were his purpose and life.

I honestly didn't know how he would react.

"Monty," I said under my breath, "are they all dead and just don't know it?"

Monty shook his head.

"Grey is quite thick-skinned and secure in who he is," Monty said. "Even at the height of their powers, the Night Wardens have never been highly regarded. They were always considered the black sheep of the magical community. I doubt he values the opinion of one magistrate regarding his purpose and life as a Night Warden."

I let out a sigh of relief.

"So this won't escalate into a bloody massacre?"

"Well, I didn't say *that*," Monty said, glancing at me. "He is also extremely protective of the Night Wardens, being one of the last, and ushering in the next generation. He will not tolerate having them disparaged."

"So, LD's concern—?"

"Is valid," Monty said. "Still, we must let this play out. I trust Grey will show restraint."

"What about his blade?"

Monty's expression darkened.

"If Izanami surfaces, everyone on that street is a corpse," Monty said, gripping the railing hard and looking down at

Grey. "It's only a matter of when. We would have to fight to bring Grey back and wrest control from her. I do not relish that scenario."

Grey chuckled and my blood froze.

"Monty?" I said. "That laugh didn't sound good."

"Because it wasn't," Monty said. "Emeric, in his ignorance, may have taken things too far."

"Meaningless existence?" Grey asked, as his voice vibrated and shifted with another voice under his. A decidedly feminine voice. "Care to clarify your statement, human?"

"Bloody hell," Monty said under his breath. "That is not good."

"*Mierda,*" I heard LD curse beneath us as he moved forward. "Grey, you need to stop."

"What is going on?" I asked, suddenly taken off-guard. "What happened?"

"Grey hasn't given Izanami total control, but he has given her some free rein," Monty said, his voice grim. "I don't know if he can retain complete control over her while he is in this state. She is quite powerful."

"So is he."

Monty stared at me.

"That's like saying you can control Kali if she decides to go on a rampage," he said. "What are the odds of that happening?"

"Zero," I said. "Is he in danger of losing it? Do we need to get down there and stop him?"

"Not yet. Besides, if she has control, the only one in danger would be whoever tried to approach him right now," he said. "We still have to let this play out. The only one who has a chance of helping Grey is LD. For now, we must not interfere."

"We're just going to watch?"

"I didn't say that," Monty snapped. "I said we must not

interfere. We will take precautions, and we will ready our weapons, though I don't know what would happen if Ebonsoul encountered Darkspirit in an actual clash, and I'm not eager to find out. There are too many variables at play here. We prepare and we stay back."

"Night Wardens are obsolete and useless," Emeric continued. "You should have been disbanded long ago and the entire group retired...permanently."

"Who was going to do this retiring?" Grey asked. "The Grand Council?"

"Step aside and allow me to execute my official duties as a magistrate of the Grand Council, Warden," Emeric demanded. "Or do you intend to stand with these rogue outcasts and end your life on this dirty street?"

Emeric looked from left to right.

"Actually," Emeric continued, "this would be a fitting place to end the last Night Warden."

Grey focused on Emeric and let out a small laugh, which jangled all of my nerves and released all of the red flags. There was no way that laughter came from Grey. Izanami had stepped on stage and she was enjoying every moment.

The magistrate didn't know what he was facing.

"It's very gracious of you to offer me a choice, Magistrate," Grey said, his voice sounding slightly off. "I think, tonight, my goals align with the outcasts."

"Very well," Emeric said, glancing at his Sanitizers. "Kill him and bring me the rogues."

As one, the Sanitizers began to move.

EIGHTEEN

Chaos descended on the street in the next few seconds.

A swarm of black orbs of energy appeared in the semi-circle of Sanitizers. I recognized them instantly. These were more of those acid orbs that melted the wall in the garage.

Another group of Sanitizers, standing behind the ones with the orbs, drew black blades covered in pulsing red runes. Behind the second group stood Emeric, his gaze focused on Grey.

Silence descended on the street and then I heard the low laughter.

"How I've relished these moments. The seconds before death is unleashed are like a balm to my dark soul."

I didn't recognize the voice. I looked around, and then realized the voice was coming from Grey.

Izanami.

"Grey," LD said closing in on him. "You can't do—"

"Stay your hand mage," Izanami said, as Grey turned to face LD. "I have not usurped control from the Warden. I do this with his blessing."

Grey smiled at that last word.

LD stopped in his tracks and stared hard at Grey.

"You in there, Grey?" LD asked. "I would really hate to have to stomp you into unconsciousness, hombre."

Grey looked at LD and smiled again.

"That you think you could, on your own, is ambitious, and misguided," Izanami said, with another smile as Grey pointed to the High Line. "Stand clear. I will not be held responsible for any harm that befalls you."

"Don't you dare hurt him," LD said, moving back and forming several gray orbs around his body. "I will take you down if I have to."

"Of course you will," Izanami said as Grey turned back to Emeric. "Magistrate, I have been instructed to give you an opportunity to surrender. Do you wish to acquiesce?"

"Surrender?" Emeric mocked as he raised his voice. "Do you know who I am? I am the magistrate to Emissary Dubois of the Grand Council. You are nothing. Less than nothing. I will accept death before ever surrendering to you."

"You think you *know* me?" Izanami said. "I roamed these planes when your kind worshipped beings like me."

"Worshipped beings like you?" Emeric jeered. "You're delusional."

"Is it possible the magistrate doesn't know about Izanami?" I asked Monty. "Because he's about to enter a world of pain."

"Grey's condition is not common knowledge," Monty said, gesturing as LD arrived next to us and threw up a silver shield. "We need to move back. Make sure your creature remains next to you at all times."

Peaches gave off a low rumble, I grabbed him by the scruff and patted his side. He stepped closer to me.

Izanami laughed again.

"Magistrate, I will leave you for last," Izanami said. "You will watch the rest of your minions die for your impudence.

"You're nothing but a broken-down, gutter-trash mage, running the streets as he wastes his life, dying a slow death," Emeric answered drawing a black blade of his own. "Have you lost your mind? My Sanitizers are doing you and the world a favor by destroying you." He looked at the Sanitizers in the semicircle of death. "What are you waiting for? Kill him!"

Grey formed a small black and silver orb. It was about the size of his palm, and hovered a few inches above his hand.

Apparently, the Sanitizers must have sensed something Emeric didn't, because their hesitation lasted a few more seconds before one, then another, and another orb, raced at Grey. In moments, I counted no less than ten black acid orbs speeding toward Grey.

Grey tapped the small orb above his hand with a finger, sending it up into the sky, and gestured. Black symbols surrounded him as the acid orbs attempted to crash into him as one.

The orbs never reached him.

The symbols around his body stopped the acid orbs before they hit him. They hovered in the air inches from him as he reached into his coat and pulled out Darkspirit.

"That can't be good," I said. "Monty? LD?"

"Can't go down there now, hombre," LD said, shaking his head. "That's not Grey. We try to tangle with a goddess and it's going to end badly...for us."

"We're just going to let her—?"

"Yes," Monty said. "Grey knows what he's doing, I hope. We can't stop Izanami, at least not right now. When Grey regains control we can try and help him."

"What is he doing with those acid orbs?" I asked. "How did he—?"

"He's ending them," LD said, his voice hard. "The magistrate made it clear, death over surrender. Grey is giving him what he wanted."

With a flick of his wrist, Grey reversed the direction of the acid orbs. They crossed the distance to the Sanitizers faster than my eyes could track.

One moment they were hovering next to Grey, the next they were punching into the Sanitizers who had sent them, disintegrating their bodies.

The screams didn't last long. It's hard to scream when acid melts your lungs and, well, your everything.

The next group of Sanitizers moved in, a little more cautious after seeing what happened to the first group. It seemed that they had more confidence, since they weren't attacking with orbs.

Their confidence was misplaced.

Grey with Izanami was fearsome and unstoppable.

The Sanitizers lunged and slashed, trying to score a hit on him. They might as well have tried to attack the air. Every time it looked like he was going to be impaled, Grey would parry, side step, duck, or jump out of the way.

The Sanitizers couldn't land one blow on him.

The same couldn't be said for Grey.

He systematically cut them down. Every time a Sanitizer tried to attack, Grey made them pay with a cut, slash, or thrust. At first, his responses weren't lethal, but that changed quickly.

After a few minutes, Sanitizers began falling after clashing with Grey. They would step away with severe wounds, walk several feet and then collapse.

In a very short amount of time, only the magistrate was left alive.

"I did promise, I would leave you for last," Izanami said. "You desired death over surrender. I am more than willing to fulfill your request."

"You think I will allow you to take my life?" Emeric

seethed. "You are not worthy to face me in battle. I will not die on this street with filth."

Grey paused, looking around at what remained of the Sanitizers.

"You would sacrifice your men to die a senseless death?"

"They live and die to serve the Grand Council," Emeric said, moving back toward the van. "The deaths were honorable, something you will never achieve." Emeric pointed his sword at Grey and gestured with his other hand. "Know this, once the rogues have been dealt with, the Grand Council will settle accounts with you—Night Warden."

"Leaving so soon?" Grey said and slashed a hand down. "Face me, Magistrate."

It was too late.

The orb Grey had pushed into the sky above him earlier, slammed into the van, flattening it with a *thump*. Grey stepped over to what remained of the van but the magistrate had escaped.

LD jumped over the railing and approached Grey, followed by Monty and me. Peaches blinked in next to me as we reached Grey.

"Grey?" LD said. "Are we good?"

"No, not really," Grey said. "Casting like that is always a bad idea."

I looked around and realized Darkspirit was gone.

"Izanami?" Monty asked. "Is she?"

"Under control," Grey said as he staggered over to the corner and sat on the curb, looking around. "Damn it, I lost my coffee. I really liked that mug."

"She's really under control?" LD asked. "How?"

"We have an understanding," Grey said, chilling me with the same words the Morrigan used to explain our agreement. "She does as I say and she gets to stay with me. If she doesn't, she gets to look for a new vessel. Took her a long time to find me. She doesn't want to go through that again, and I enjoy breathing. Win-win for everyone."

"Where did the magistrate go?" I asked. "Can we track him?"

"You won't have to," Grey said. "He's regrouping. Did you sense the teleportation spike, Tea and Crumpets?"

Monty nodded.

"Teleportation spike?" I asked. "What teleportation spike?"

"A massive energy spike surged several blocks from here," Monty said looking south. "I can only assume it's the magistrate with reinforcements."

"If they come this way, I'll slow them down—" Grey started.

"You'll slow down nothing," LD said. "You weren't even supposed to be involved in this fight. You were here to give us a place to meet off the grid."

"That wasn't too successful," Grey said, slurring some of his words. "We should have used the Hellfire."

"Can't," LD said. "Edict affects them and Erik would have a fit if you showed up there and started a brawl."

"He is way too high strung," Grey said. "I didn't get too involved."

"Involved enough," LD said. "You better believe the Grand Council is going to look into you after this."

"Only if the Emissary isn't convinced that would be a bad idea," Grey said looking at Monty and me then holding his head. "My headache is going to be epic."

"Serves you right," LD said. "You should've stayed out of it."

"Ten business only?" Grey asked with a lopsided grin. "I'll be fine after a gallon or two of my Death Wish. I think I'm going to need a nap, too."

"That's your car over there, right?" LD asked as he pointed to the Dark Goat parked on the far corner. "Yes?"

"Yes," I said. "But we can't leave you and Grey here alone—"

"You can and you will," LD said, reaching into his jacket, pulling out a small glowing book, and handing it to Monty. "You want into the Ten? This is where your initiation starts. Your reason for meeting me here is in that book. Make sure you don't lose it. That book is a key to where you're going."

"What are you saying?" I asked. "We have to face the magistrate alone?"

"You are never alone, Strong," LD said. "You should know that by now. However, you do have to deal with, not only the magistrate, but—"

"The Emissary as well," Monty finished. "We have to convince him to stop this edict, don't we?"

"Or die trying," LD said with a tight smile. "The magistrate isn't a coward, he was trying to get you two to make a move. Don't fall for his traps. He effectively removed this stubborn dinosaur."

He glanced down at Grey.

"I don't understand," I said. "What do you mean?"

"I wish you had the time for me to explain it to you, but you don't," he said. "Get moving, the magistrate is coming and he is bringing more expendables. You can't be here when he arrives."

"Where are you going?" I asked. "You're not going to stay and fight?"

"Wish I could, but I have to get Grey to safety," LD said. "You have your next location there." He pointed to the book Monty held. "I'm leaving you in good hands, some of the best. I was supposed to give you a thorough debrief, but you know how it goes in our life. Situations are in flux—always."

"Good hands?" I asked, looking around. "I'm not seeing

any good hands; I'm not seeing *any* hands. Whose hands? Where are these hands?"

"Strong," LD said, interrupting me. "Take a breath. I know it looks bad, but it's not worse than anything you've faced."

"We've never faced the Grand Council."

"You have a point there, but it's not *much* worse than anything you've faced," LD agreed. "Don't let fear shape your thoughts. Think about what you're facing and why."

"From where I'm standing, it's much, much worse," I said. "Can you at least tell us where we're supposed to go?"

"Not out here," LD said, looking around. "The Grand Council has some excellent resources. It's better if they find out when you do." He pointed to the book he gave Monty. "There's a reason it's in the book. If it were a matter of just telling you, TK would have."

"The Emissary must have a plan," Monty said. "We are not the end goal. We can't be. There is something we aren't seeing."

"Plenty," LD said, getting Grey to his feet. "At least one of you is thinking. If you figure out what the Emissary wants, you figure out his plan. Don't fall for the misdirections, don't let him goad you, and watch that magistrate; he is cunning and clever. Do *not* underestimate him. Now get going."

LD gestured and formed a silver circle under both himself and Grey. The next second, they were gone.

We ran to the Dark Goat.

NINETEEN

By the time we reached the Dark Goat, I heard the roar of engines behind us.

Peaches had blinked into the car, claiming his backseat kingdom with an expansive sprawl, while Monty and I jumped into our seats and strapped in.

"Why does that sound like more than a van?" I asked, turning on the engine with a roar. "How many reinforcements did Emeric get?"

"Would you like to remain here and count them when they arrive?" Monty asked. "I believe they are fairly close."

"No, thanks," I said. "Look in that book and find out where we're supposed to go. Can't believe LD couldn't just tell us."

"I'm sure they have their reasons," Monty said. "Speed is of the essence. Our chances of survival increase exponentially if we make ourselves a moving target."

I floored the gas and sped uptown.

As Monty opened the book, several symbols I couldn't understand floated out of the book and into the Dark Goat, hovering slowly around us. A second later, a thin golden beam shot into the air, right through the roof and into the night sky. It remained with us as we raced down the street.

"What the hell is that?" I asked. The beam remained steady as we raced uptown on 10th Avenue. "What is that beam doing?"

Monty focused on the hovering signals around us, peering at some and touching some of the others. He slowly maneuvered them around the interior, ignoring the fact that we were broadcasting our location to the entire Grand Council death squad behind us.

"Fascinating," he whispered, mostly to himself. "These seem to be connected to some kind of summoning ritual."

"Summoning ritual? Who or what exactly are we summoning?"

"I don't know," Monty said, still focused on the symbols. "These are proto-runes. I can make out some of them, but the context is missing. What little I can make out speaks to a formation of darkness."

"The fleet of angry Grand Council death mobiles wasn't enough?"

"I doubt the formation of darkness alludes to our current pursuers," he said, glancing behind us again. "This speaks to something else. As I said the context is missing, but I hardly think LD would give us the means to attract *more* Grand Council minions to our location."

"Why would he need to do that? We're doing fantastic on our own."

"I must be misreading the symbols," Monty said. "Perhaps I'm seeing the formation of darkness too literally?"

"Formation of darkness?" I said more than slightly alarmed. "We just summoned a formation of darkness? What formation of darkness? Made up of what? Is this beam some sort of bat-signal?"

"According to these symbols, it appears you're not too far

off," Monty said, glancing behind us. "We have substantial company."

I looked in the rear-view mirror and saw a sea of headlights.

Peaches rumbled behind me and let out a low growl. He shifted out of his sprawl and turned to face the back to look out the rear window.

"I feel you, boy," I said. "But we can't go out there and bite them right now."

"Keep your creature close," Monty said. "There appears to be more information in this book."

"Is that symbol giving away our location?" I asked, glancing into the rear-view mirror. "Who assembled the street racing brigade?"

"I would hazard to guess these are the reinforcements LD mentioned," Monty said, turning the pages of the book. "We need to make sure we are not apprehended."

"Oh, that's the plan?" I asked, swerving around some traffic. "Make sure they don't catch us. That's some next-level strategy there. Don't get caught?"

"Yes, don't get caught and head to...this...this *must* be a mistake," Monty said, turning the pages and then back again as he read. "No one has used that tunnel since the war. I thought it had been collapsed."

"What tunnel? What are you talking about? Where are we going, Monty, and why are you calling it a mistake?"

"According to our instructions, we are to proceed to Governor's Island," Monty said. "It must be a mistake, because—"

"Governor's Island is exactly that, an island, and the last time I checked, the Dark Goat can do some amazing things, but turning into a boat or a sub isn't one of them," I said, keeping one eye on the road and one eye on the closing swarm of vehicles behind us. "Are those? What exactly *are* they driving?"

"It looks like imports, Japanese imports to be precise," Monty said after a glance behind us. "They are driving Subaru Impreza WRXs. I would imagine they have some modifications to increase speed and durability. I'm fairly certain these are not SuNaTran vehicles."

"Cecil doesn't work on imports?"

"If I recall correctly, you managed to convert a Lamborghini Aventador into expressionist art," Monty said without turning his gaze from the rear. "Cecil has no compunctions about working on foreign vehicles, no. He just won't do work for the Grand Council...ever."

"First, I didn't destroy the Aventador," I said, insulted. "Cecil needs to let that go. It was Gren the Troll. Remember him?"

"Vividly," Monty answered. "Unfortunately, our current pursuers won't be as easy to dispatch."

"Why won't Cecil work on Grand Council vehicles?" I asked, dodging a bus and nearly scraping the side of the Dark Goat on a truck. "Something to do with them being insane and issuing death sentences?"

"The Fairchilds and Montagues have many arrangements, as you know," Monty explained. "A mutual dislike for the Grand Council and most authority in general is a commonality they both share."

"They can't force him?" I asked, sliding between two cars, stopping short to avoid rear ending another, and increasing my speed again to pass another taxi. "He can defy them?"

"He's a Fairchild with vast resources," Monty answered. "They cannot force him to do anything he doesn't want to do."

I glanced in the rear-view mirror again.

"I can't believe the Grand Council is using Japanese imports. Why?"

"The Grand Council is a worldwide organization—costs, easy modifications and runic kits, in addition to durability... I'm sure there is a branch of the Grand Council in Japan that facilitates their exportation."

I glanced at Monty and shook my head.

"Rhetorical," I said. "I don't really care why they're driving samurai slammers, but if they're modded, I don't know how long we can keep outrunning them. Damn, they're fast. Which is irrelevant because you still haven't told me how I am supposed to *drive* the Dark Goat to Governor's Island?"

"There is a way, but we can't drive the entire way there."

"Does that have something to do with all of the *water* between us and Governor's Island?"

"No, the water is irrelevant," Monty said. "There *is* a tunnel, but it hasn't been in use, at least not to my knowledge, for decades."

"There is no tunnel to Governor's Island, Monty," I said. "I know my city and I know for a fact there is no tunnel that leads directly to Governor's Island."

"I didn't say directly."

"Not even indirectly," I said, getting upset. "There is no tunnel, so you better have a backup site or something, because we're not getting there unless the Dark Goat has a submarine function. Did Cecil install a submarine function I don't know about?"

"I don't believe Cecil planned on an abundance of nautical adventures for this vehicle," Monty said. "To my knowledge, there are no submarine functions on this vehicle. This is not the Mobula."

"A simple no," I said, trying to keep the roaring fleet of

vehicles behind us. "It's not that hard. Why Governor's Island?"

"There is a tunnel, but it's not known or available to the public at large," he said. "It's not designed for vehicles. We will have to make our way there on foot, but I can assist with that. Before you ask, teleportation is out of the question, even, I think, for your creature."

"Where exactly is this tunnel, in Hades?"

"Much closer than that," Monty said. "Hard right!"

I pulled the wheel hard to the right and avoided a large black orb that held an oppressive and murderous energy signature. The orb slammed into a parked car, barely missing the Dark Goat. The car instantly started melting into a pool of sludge. Flashbacks of the Goat being melted surfaced immediately in my mind.

"Did they just try to melt us?" I asked, raising my voice. "What the actual fu—?"

"The Grand Council has made its intentions clear," Monty said, cutting me off. "We need to take them seriously. They present a credible threat. At least the magistrate does."

"I took him seriously when he exploded our home, through the defensive runes," I said, angrily. "Now I want to take him and the rest of these Sanitizers out of play."

"We don't have the time to engage them all," Monty said. "Their numbers give them the advantage. We need to head to the Hugh L. Carey Tunnel. That orb was particularly potent."

"Potent?" I said, as a mix of anger and fear rose inside me. I really didn't want to see if the Dark Goat could survive a direct hit, but if we stayed on the street long enough we *were* going to get hit. "That's one way to describe it. How about, that magistrate is a homicidal maniac? What if someone had been in that car? He could've killed someone."

"I believe that's the goal, with the someone in question being us."

"Don't you have an anti-acid cast or something?" I asked. "Something to prevent massive melting from one of those orbs?"

"Are you requesting an antacid cast?" he asked glancing at me. "Is your stomach in distress?"

"You know what has me in distress? That you think this is the right time to break out the mage humor," I said. "That has me in distress."

He almost smiled and shook his head.

"We're moving too fast to mount an effective defense against a cast like that," he said. "The best counter to those orbs is not to get hit."

I nodded and gripped the wheel harder.

Tonight was not the night this magistrate melted us or the Dark Goat. I wasn't going to let that happen.

"If that thing had hit us, would we have survived?"

"I don't know and I would prefer not to find out."

"That wasn't some regular Sanitizer acid orb," I said. "Even I could feel the power that orb had. It was much stronger than the one that melted the wall at the Moscow."

Monty gave me a short nod.

"Which leads me to believe it was the magistrate who cast it," he answered. "Get us to the Hugh L. Carey Tunnel. I will attempt to deflect his orbs, now that I know what to sense for."

"No one calls it the Hugh L. Carey anything," I corrected, swerving out of my lane to make it harder for the magistrate to hit us with another of those acid orbs. "You mean the Brooklyn Battery Tunnel?"

"Yes, yes," Monty said, his voice tense. "Keep your eyes on the road, and get us there as soon as you can. We need to get off this street."

We had just crossed 30th Street and 10th, chased by a

small fleet of ten to fifteen cars, several vans, and what looked like two armored trucks.

We headed north on 10th Avenue and the entrance to the Brooklyn Battery Tunnel was at the southern tip of the island. The end of the southbound West Side Highway led straight into the tunnel.

"You realize that tunnel is *behind* us?"

"I'm aware," Monty said, pointing ahead. "There, on 34th, make a left and head west." He glanced down at the book and traced a symbol in the air in front of him. It left a white afterimage as he moved his fingers through the air. "If I'm reading this section of the book correctly, I think I'm beginning to understand what LD meant about leaving us in good hands."

"Glad someone understands what's going on," I grumbled as I accelerated for the next two blocks. "Hold on, this is going to be a rough turn."

I kept the gas pedal floored as the Dark Goat roared ahead.

In the next few seconds, I understood what LD meant.

TWENTY

We barely made the turn onto 34th Street.

The Dark Goat held together, hugging the corner as we rounded the turn and shot forward. I really thought we would either flip or break something because of our speed.

I shook my head as we cleared the corner and raced across town. Under my breath, I whispered a silent prayer to Cecil for all of his automotive and runic skills.

Some of the Grand Council's vehicles could've used Cecil's expertise as I heard several of them collide with each other along with the parked cars on the street, as the fleet of vehicles rounded the corner in pursuit. There were now fewer cars chasing us, but they were closing the distance. There was no way we would make the West Side Highway before they pounced on us.

I was about to tell Monty we needed another plan. Something that involved him unleashing a massive orb of destruction on the Grand Council.

That's when the earth exploded behind us.

The Dark Goat became airborne for a few seconds before bouncing several times and skidding to the side. I fought to keep her straight as she sideswiped a couple of parked cars, smashing them into unrecognizable abstract automotive art before I overcompensated and slid to the other side of 34th Street.

We came to a stop after a few more seconds of drifting.

Behind us 34th Street was now the 34th Street crater. From 10th Avenue to 11th Avenue, halfway down the block, the center of the street resembled a very large bowl. Monty got out as I turned the engine on again.

I didn't know what had just arrived, but there was no way I was going to meet whatever decided to join this dance and not have a way to get out of Dodge in a hurry.

"What was that?" I asked, jumping out of the Dark Goat. "It nearly hit us."

"Not what, who," Monty said. "Formation of darkness, I translated it wrong. The actual meaning is—"

Now I knew what that beam summoned.

"Midnight Echelon," I said, as I looked into the center of the crater and saw two figures. One I recognized immediately. She was a giant of a woman dressed in black combat armor, built for maximum carnage. She had large black wings unfurled behind her and held a massive, oversized battle-axe covered in black energy.

Nan.

The axe she held was named Stormchaser and was nearly as scary as Dex's Nemain. Next to her was another woman who was nearly as fearsome though not as large. I doubted anyone was as large as Nan. This woman's black and gray combat armor sent a clear message.

Step before me and die.

At first glance, it appeared she didn't carry a weapon, but thinking that would be a mistake. Gauntlets covered in spikes and flowing black energy encased her hands.

Braun.

If Nan was built for maximum carnage, Braun's entire purpose was pain distribution of epic proportions. Nan and Braun both jumped out of the crater at the same time, except Nan jumped toward us, landing next to Peaches, and Braun jumped out on the opposite side.

To intercept the Grand Council convoy.

"What is she doing?" I asked, as Braun started a slow jog toward the fleet of vehicles headed her way. "They'll crush her!"

"If she allows such a small group of vehicles to cause her harm, she is undeserving of being in the Midnight Echelon," Nan said. "Sadly, we cannot stay to watch her do battle, much as I would enjoy the spectacle. We have other matters to attend to."

"Other matters to attend to?" I asked, looking past her at the oncoming Grand Council and pointing. "That's the Grand Council."

"Braun has been instructed to leave the magistrate alive," Nan said with a glance back. "Against her wishes. We must fly, there are more reinforcements on the way. Verity has sent a sizable contingent of mages to deal with you. It appears you have made quite the impression."

"Verity?" I asked. "Why am I not surprised?"

"The Grand Council must be using their mages," Monty said. "If Verity is joining this pursuit, we will be overrun in seconds."

"We are not without our own resources," Nan said. "Right now, the priority is to leave this place. Braun will hold them here."

"Alone?" I asked. "I mean, I know she is powerful. She's going to do this alone?"

"I admit it will be somewhat difficult, she will refrain from ending their lives," Nan said with a nod. "It will require restraint. Braun has some difficulty with restraint."

"Somewhat difficult?"

"You have done well," Nan said, clapping me on the shoulder with a massive hand. "A large amount of enemies wish for your demise with great fervor. This is good."

I stared at her for a few seconds.

"Where I come from, that is not a good thing."

"It is where I'm from," she said, glancing at Monty and Peaches "Well met, Mage Montague and Mighty One."

"Well met, Nan," Monty said, with a short bow. "Now I understand what LD meant about leaving us in good hands."

Nan nodded as she rubbed Peaches' head.

"I will take you to the mouth of the tunnel," Nan said, walking west. "You will leave your vehicle here. The next part of your journey will require you to travel on foot." She glanced at Monty. "You understand the path, Mage? You cannot teleport there."

Monty nodded. We started following her as she picked up the pace.

"No teleportation to Governor's Island," Monty said. "We must use the ventilation access from the Hugh L. Carey Tunnel to gain entry onto the island."

"Correct," she said, glancing at Peaches. "The Mighty One will follow. I will not carry all three of you."

Peaches let out a low rumble followed by a low bark.

"Once we reach the tunnel," she continued, "I will collapse the entrance. You will have to find another exit from the island once all this is over."

"You're going to collapse the tunnel?" I asked, surprised. "This is a major tunnel in the city."

"The *entrance*, not the entire tunnel," Nan corrected. "This will force any of the Grand Council not on the island to use sea vessels to gain access. The tunnel will be closed."

"Won't that create too much attention?"

"The Bear will handle the repairs and city authorities,"

Nan said. "I am told your battles in this city have given her much experience in dealing with disasters of this sort."

"That wasn't us," I protested reflexively. "Wait a minute, the Bear?"

"Ursula," Monty said. "DAMNED will handle the tunnel entrance collapse as one of their cleanup projects, creating a cover for the destruction."

I nodded as it made sense.

I hadn't even thought of Ursula and the DAMNED as being on our side, but they were outcasts too, in their own way. I would have to get her and her crew something special for standing with us. Maybe a special hammer warmer for those cold winter nights out on the streets.

Nan absorbed her battle-axe and extended both arms as she broke into a run. I was having trouble keeping up with her, which shouldn't have been possible, since she was wearing combat armor that looked like it weighed an easy two hundred pounds, if not more.

"To me," she said. "We must leave this place with haste."

Monty and I each grabbed a hand. With a flap of her wings, she became airborne. We stayed low, but blazed over the West Side Highway at speed. I saw Peaches blink out and reappear beneath us a few seconds later. I thought the Dark Goat was fast; traveling by Valkyrie Express was faster.

I don't know how she stayed airborne with all that armor and the additional weight of two adults, but she got us to the entrance of the Brooklyn Battery Tunnel in less than five minutes. Peaches kept pace and joined us at the entrance when we landed.

I noticed there were construction barricades in place and large orange signs indicating that the tunnel was closed due to ongoing repairs. LD had prepped this beforehand with Ursula's help.

I looked around but saw no sign of Ursula or the

DAMNED. I guessed they would be on the scene after Nan renovated the entrance, trapping us inside the tunnel.

"There's one more thing," Nan said as we started for the entrance to the tunnel. "There is the small matter of your battle name, Strong."

I turned to face her and had to look up.

"Battle name? What's wrong with my name?" I asked. "I like my name."

"You have fought alongside the Midnight Echelon and survived," Nan said, forming her battle-axe. "Simon Strong does not convey the necessary fear to those who would stand against you."

"'Lucky to be alive' doesn't work as a name either," I said. "Simon Strong is my name."

"Not in the Midnight Echelon," she said with a headshake. "You need something that will make your foes tremble. A true battle name."

"I leave the inducing fear to people like you, Monty, and my hellhound."

Nan shook her head.

"That will not do," she said, serious. "This naming was given to me. It is my honor and responsibility."

"You do realize I already have a name?"

"Not a battle name," she said. "I will give you one now."

Because there are moments when my brain doesn't get the memo before my mouth kicks into gear I said the next words.

"Are you saying I don't get a say in my own name?"

She slowly shook her head and crossed her arms.

"No, you do not," she said, peering down at me. "Only the pretentious or deluded name themselves."

"You know, Nan isn't exactly fear-inducing," I said. "I mean, what do *your* enemies say when they hear you're coming? Oh no, it's Nan! Not exactly up there in the pee my pants from fear department."

Monty stared at me and wisely took a few steps back, probably to be outside of the arc of her swing, in case she wanted to bury Stormchaser in my chest, in some special Midnight Echelon lesson of pain, death, and discretion.

She smiled and my blood decided to freeze in place.

"Those few of my enemies who can overcome their fear to speak when they hear of my presence on the battlefield, only do so to curse their existence, knowing they will face me in their last moments of life, or beg for a quick death. Usually both," she said. "The rest do, in fact, soil themselves from fear."

And because the memo still hadn't reached the functioning parts of my brain, I decided to keep speaking, because why not live dangerously by pissing off a giant, axe-wielding Dark Valkyrie?

"And *you* don't think Simon Strong does that?"

She narrowed her eyes at me.

"It does *not*," she said, staring at me with a look that dared me to contradict her. "I will use the name the Warden Mage has given you. From this moment forth, the Midnight Echelon will address you as Deathless."

"Deathless?" I asked, glancing at Monty, who nodded. Nan paused and shot me a look that explained there was no choice in this, not even the *illusion* of a choice, and if I ever thought there was, I needed to take that thought, crush it to a fine powder and then scatter that powder into the wind. "Right, Deathless. Isn't that a little on the nose?"

"No, it fits," she said. "It is a name you can grow into like the Mighty Peaches has. Over time, you will be called by this name and it will serve you well. Mark my words."

I nodded solemnly.

She nodded back, took another breath, and rested Stormchaser on my shoulder. To say I was a bit nervous about having her battle-axe inches away from my neck, would've been the understatement of the century.

It was a great incentive to let her speak.

"If you say so," I managed, warily eyeing her battle-axe. "I'm sure it will grow on me."

She nodded again.

"Let your enemies tremble at the mention of this name," she started. "Let the sound of your name rob them of their sleep and peace. Let this name strike fear in all who would oppose you and those who stand by your side. The name Deathless will be whispered as a curse by your enemies and as a prayer by those you protect. So says Hanna the Horror of the Midnight Echelon."

I had so many things to say at the mention of her full battle name, but somehow the battle-axe resting on my shoulder advised me that Billy Shakes was right on this one: discretion is the better part of valor.

I kept my mouth shut and she stepped back.

"Thank you," Monty said. "We will take it from here. How soon until the magistrate arrives?"

Nan looked up into the sky.

"No more than twenty minutes," she said. "If Braun is feeling merciful. She does get carried away, which is why I must return. We don't need her accidentally crushing everyone there with her fists. Do you understand the instructions?"

"Survive until the Emissary appears," Monty said. "Then survive his initial onslaught."

"Your focus will be the magistrate," she said, hefting the battle-axe onto her shoulder. "The old man will deal with the Emissary but do not underestimate the magistrate. He is a dangerous foe, Banshee."

Monty nodded as she rubbed Peaches' head.

"Understood," he said. "We will follow the instructions."

"I certainly hope you do," she said and pointed to the interior of the tunnel with her weapon. "May the blood of your enemies be a soothing balm to your blades."

"May the cry of battle ring loud in your ears," Monty said, placing a fist over his heart and giving her a short bow.

"Well spoken, mage," Nan said, returning the salute. "Off with you."

We ran into the tunnel.

We were a hundred yards in when I saw Nan take several massive swings at the stones forming the entrance of the Brooklyn Battery Tunnel.

In minutes, instead of the double arches leading into the city, we were faced with a mountain of rubble.

"How long will that hold them?"

"Not very long," Monty answered. "We need to move. Emeric and what remains of the Grand Council will be coming through here shortly. This rubble will be an annoyance at best."

TWENTY-ONE

"One moment," he said. "This should facilitate our traversing the tunnel and reaching our destination with haste."

Monty turned to me and began gesturing.

Golden symbols flowed from his fingers, descending gently onto me. In seconds I felt invigorated. My body felt charged and full of energy.

"Whoa," I said. "What *is* that? It's almost as good as javambrosia."

"It's a life-force transmutation cast," he said, explaining exactly nothing as I gave him a look. "It takes a person's life force and converts it to a short-term burst of energy. You're feeling a heightened reaction due to your particular condition."

"How long does this last?"

"For someone not cursed alive? Ten to fifteen minutes," Monty said. "For you? I'm not sure. To be on the safe side, we'll reassess where you are once we reach the ventilation access."

He gestured again and the same symbols fell on him. He

stretched his back and shook his hands out as he twisted his body left and right.

"That is refreshing," he said, cracking his neck. "How are you feeling?"

"Like I could run a marathon in about ten minutes flat," I said. "This is great and everything, but why can't we teleport to Governor's Island? Wouldn't that be faster?"

"You recall the defenses on Ellis Island," Monty asked, "making it a runic prison?"

"I remember," I said with a nod. "Are you saying Governor's Island is the same?"

"No," Monty said with a head shake. "Governor's Island is ten times worse."

"What?"

"The Island, which is no longer in use, is a designated mage Stronghold," he said. "At its height of use, a mage couldn't cast anywhere on the island. Even the most minor cast was impossible. It was the ultimate neutral zone."

"Are those defenses still in place?"

"No, we're talking centuries ago," Monty said. "However, it's still an island and the Stronghold runes still exist. Teleporting there without a circle would be dangerous."

"Let's pass on the dangerous teleport," I said. "I like my insides, inside."

"Agreed," he said. "The major effect we have to concern ourselves with now is the one every island presents—the flowing water around the island obstructing the casts. Ready?"

I nodded.

"Ready," I said, stretching my back. "How fast do you want to—?"

He took off, leaving me to stare at his back.

"Do try to keep up," he said, his voice trailing off as he motored down the tunnel. I'd never seen Monty run that fast, not even when creatures were trying to shred us to pieces. "Let's go, Deathless!"

"What the hell?" I said, looking from my hellhound to back down the tunnel in shock. "He left us in the dust." I patted my hellhound's ginormous head. "Let's go catch him."

I took off at a dead run as Peaches blinked out next to me and reappeared about ten feet in front of me. I picked up the pace and felt my body glide along the tunnel with ease. I nearly fell over a few times because it was too easy to move so fast.

I had to recalibrate where my center of gravity rested as I adjusted to the increased velocity. Once I became comfortable with my new speed, I increased the pace. In the distance, I kept seeing Peaches blinking in and out.

There was no way I would ever catch up to him, but I *was* gaining on Monty. In a few seconds, I would overtake him.

Then he disappeared.

I skidded to a stop and retraced my steps.

There were no doors or access ways where I had seen him vanish. I looked carefully and still I saw nothing out of the ordinary. A few seconds later Peaches appeared next to me.

<This way bondmate.>
<Where did you go?>
<Inside the wall. There is a way.>
<Inside the wall?>
<This way. The angry man said to get you.>
<Which way?>

Peaches stepped to the edge of the roadway and then moved around a corner out of sight, into a small corridor. There, he edged closer to the wall and then vanished. He came back, just his head, and then disappeared again.

I followed him, extending my arm first and watching it disappear into the wall. I kept walking and found myself in a narrow corridor, barely wide enough for both of us to walk side by side.

The corridor was made of the same tile as the rest of the tunnel, but this tile was covered in softly glowing violet runes. I didn't understand what they said, but I could tell they were ancient.

<You were very fast. Have you been eating more meat? If you keep eating meat, you can be even faster. Then you can run with me.>

<Run with you? I don't think I can ever be that fast. I don't know if I want to be that fast. I would probably crash into walls every few seconds if I moved that fast.>

<If you ate enough meat it wouldn't hurt. Much.>

Meat was apparently the solution to everything, according to my Zen Master hellhound.

We came to the end of the narrow corridor where a large, rune-covered steel door greeted us. I could tell it was old from the hinges and the design work, but it opened easily and silently.

On the other side of the door was a vast octagonal room with stairs leading up alongside the wall. At each break in the room, at the start of another section of the octagon, the stairs would become a landing, creating eight landings, each one higher than the previous one, before reaching surface level.

Situated around the room were desks, and filing cabinets. To one side, I saw a long rectangular table with a dozen chairs around it.

On another side, I saw what looked like an enormous teleportation circle inscribed into the floor. When I stepped close to it, I realized it wasn't inscribed, but formed out of copper and embedded into the floor.

The symbols it contained, which I thought had been written in red ink, turned out to be made of ruby crystals, reflecting the light back against the walls in soft red hues.

The rest of the room was mostly empty. I could see two other doors, but those remained locked. Each of those doors were covered in some of the same ancient runic symbols.

In another part of the room, I saw an area that appeared to be a switchboard of some kind, but it seemed to predate any type of communication I was familiar with.

On a wall near the ancient switchboard was a world map with areas marked across countries covered with what looked like small, clear crystal pins.

There were too many pins to count easily, but I could make out that some of them were in clusters, forming networks.

Some of the pins were connected with a thin silver chain, while others stood alone, isolated. Still other locations were marked with a black pin, and these too, remained isolated.

Monty was waiting for us on a landing halfway up the stairs.

"What is this place?" I asked when I reached the landing Monty stood on. "It looks like some kind of war room."

"It was officially called the SMDC—Strategic Mage Deployment Command," Monty said. "Unofficially known as a SABLE Room."

"SABLE?" I asked. "What does SABLE stand for?"

"SABLE stood for—Strategic Attack Battalion Logistics and Erasures," he said. "These command rooms were used during the major conflicts for covert operations."

I looked down over the room again.

"This was a black ops command and control?" I asked. "Did you deploy out of here?"

Monty nodded.

"A few times, yes, back when it was operational," Monty said, looking down around the room. He pointed to the circle with the ruby symbols. "That circle could teleport an operative to any other SMDC around the world. Back then there were several hundred worldwide to deal with conflicts."

I scanned the room slowly.

"How is this place still intact?" I asked. "Why wasn't it scrubbed and sanitized?"

"An excellent question," Monty said, gazing around the room. "I was under the impression that it had been. Apparently I was wrong."

"You think anyone is still using it?" I asked. "Does the Grand Council know about this place?"

"No, it's no longer in use, but the Grand Council assuredly knows of its existence," Monty said. "They will follow us here."

"The room is rundown, but that circle seems like it could work."

"It seems intact, but the circle is missing its activating catalyst." He pointed to the copper circle. "See there, along the outer edge, a section is missing."

I looked at where he pointed and saw he was right. A section of the outer circle was missing a piece of copper.

"If that section was put in place, would that circle work? Even down here?"

"Theoretically," Monty said. "But where would it go? All the SMDC were decommissioned after the war. Even this one, while still intact, is non-functional. There's no personnel and no power is being fed to the circle. They require an immense amount of energy to function properly."

"Where do these stairs lead?" I asked, looking up. "Governor's Island?"

Monty nodded.

"There's a walkway that leads to the island, which contains failsafes, if it becomes compromised," Monty said. "The same applies to this room, though I doubt the failsafes would still be operational after all this time."

"Why are we headed to Governor's Island?"

"We're not," Monty said. "Not initially."

I gave him a look.

"Did one of those acid orbs bounce off your head?" I asked. "We're standing in some black ops command, above us is a ventilation access with a walkway that leads straight to Governor's Island."

"Yes, that is all true."

"What part of all that is us *not* headed to Governor's Island?" I asked, incredulous. "Because it really looks like that's what we're doing."

"We're leading Emeric and his minions to the Island, but first we have to confront him."

"Tell me we're not going to try *tact* on him," I said. "My diplomacy is broken today."

"We will engage him long enough to reactivate the island defenses," Monty said. "When I say engage, I mean antagonize."

"Excuse me?" I said. "You do realize he wants to eliminate us?"

"I'm aware."

"And you want us to do, what, exactly?" I asked. "Have a chat with him? Maybe share a cup of tea?"

"If we step immediately onto the island, I don't know if the Stronghold runes will take effect and limit my casting," Monty said, looking up. "I need to control their activation. We are heading to the walkway first. There, we will confront the magistrate."

"You want us to face the acid-orb-throwing magistrate on a walkway where we will be exposed?" I asked. "I doubt he's coming at us alone."

"Most likely not," Monty said. "There will be a sizable contingent of Sanitizers and Verity agents with him."

"That doesn't sound like a survivable strategy."

"If we remain on the walkway, it's not, but we are not staying on the walkway," he said. "We are going to force Emeric's hand into making a fatal error using every mage's greatest weakness."

"Self-absorbed, fastidious pretension, masked with a thin veil of superiority, condescension, and delusions of grandeur wrapped around a massive ego?"

He stared at me.

"Do you view *all* mages this way?"

"Only the ones who have tried to kill me," I said. "That list isn't exactly short you know, but the description is accurate."

"I was going to say his ego," he said. "You seem to have been extensively studying mages' psyches."

"It's not hidden or a secret," I answered. "Individuals, when they get power, also get predictable. Some will use it for good, and others will get all megalomaniacal, trying to destroy their enemies and take over the world. We have a tendency to attract the second group for some reason."

"We have indeed," Monty said. "I do have to agree though, mages do seem to have fragile egos."

"Not all, just most," I said. "Dex doesn't have an issue. Neither do you, really. Emeric on the other hand, his buttons are easy to push. Insult the Emissary, question his authority, or suggest that Emeric himself is inferior in some way, and you will set him off."

"You've been giving this thought."

"Ever since the Moscow, when he redecorated our home and insulted us," I said, clamping down on the anger. "He came across as a pompous ass."

"Because he is," Monty added. "That's why you're going to face him while I activate the Stronghold runes."

I rubbed my ear and shook my head.

"I'm sorry, my hearing must be going," I said. "It sounded

like you said, I was facing Emeric and you were going to activate the Stronghold runes—the same runes that will prevent you from casting—anything."

"That will prevent every mage on the island from casting. Think about what that means."

"It means you will be vulnerable," I said. "Are you insane? You can't do that."

"Extrapolate, Simon," he said. "I *will* be vulnerable, true. Every *mage* on Governor's Island will be vulnerable."

"I just said that," I said, getting upset. "Are you going deaf too?"

"Every mage will be vulnerable," he said. "Do you understand?"

"No!" I said raising my voice. "He'll tear you apart!"

Monty sighed and shook his head.

"Every mage will be defenseless, however, there are some entities,"—he glanced down at Peaches and then looked at me—"who are not mages. Their source of power should not be affected by the Stronghold runes. *They* will not be vulnerable."

Then it dawned on me.

"I'm not a mage, and neither is Peaches."

"You don't say."

"This is totally going to suck," I said. "How long before you can activate these runes?"

"That might be complicated."

"Of course it is," I said. "Let me guess, the activation area requires some secret access rune that only works when you do your special wiggle-fingers in reverse or something like that."

"One day I would really like to visit this reality you inhabit," Monty said, giving me a look. "It sounds like a fascinating place. The Stronghold runes can only be activated from the control tower."

"Which is located where exactly?"

"Inside Fort Jay, not too far from the walkway," Monty said. "That will be your fall-back point. You will need to bring Emeric there."

"And?" I asked. "I'm sensing there's more."

"I don't know what condition it's in," he said. "Or if the ley-line activator will function. I have to assume they have been inert for decades if not longer."

"And you want me to face a magistrate, who is currently getting his ass beat by an angry valkyrie, while you figure all this out?"

"He will be in the perfect frame of mind."

"What frame is that, murderous?"

"Irrational," Monty said, pulling out the book LD had given him. "The details are becoming clearer now."

The book gave off a soft golden glow.

"Is that thing going to fire another beam, giving away our location?" I asked, eyeballing the book warily. "Why is it glowing?"

"It's a key," Monty said. "That's what LD said. I didn't understand him in the moment, but this book is the key to activate the defenses on the island."

"I thought he said that book is a key, like an instruction manual," I said. "I don't think we're going to have that kind of time where you can read about how to activate the defenses."

"No, the book itself is a key," Monty said, examining the small book. "I, myself, do not possess enough power to activate the defenses. This book will make it possible."

I looked at the book.

"It doesn't seem that powerful," I said. "Are you sure it can do that? I know LD gave you the book. Do you know where he got it? Is this some relic from Fordey Boutique?"

"My uncle gave it to him," Monty said. "It seems my uncle is responsible for most of this."

"You just figured that out?" I asked. "He *stole* the Golden Circle."

"No, you don't understand, this goes beyond relocating the Golden Circle," Monty said. "He must have been planning this from the moment the Golden Circle changed the battlemage curriculum."

"No way," I said. "How could he have possibly—?"

"He precipitated this entire scenario," he said. "I hesitate to consider how long and how complex this plan of his truly is."

"I don't understand," I said. "You're saying Dex planned all of this?"

"Yes. He anticipated most of it," Monty said, glancing upward. "Then he created the framework for what he couldn't anticipate."

"He knew the Grand Council would come after us?" I asked, not entirely surprised at Dex playing ultimate 6D chess while everyone else was playing tic-tac-toe. "He knew that we would be outcasts?"

"As we've grown in power, the circles we've moved in have become smaller," Monty said. "It was only a matter of time before one of the many organizations in our world classified us as such."

"So he gave it a kickstart?" I asked. "How nice of him."

"There are layers we can't see, at least not yet," he said. "If he caused this, it's because it needed to happen."

"Needed to happen?" I said. "Really? We needed to have our home blown up? We needed melting acid orbs thrown at us? We needed a psychotic magistrate chasing us, looking to end our lives?"

"Well, it hasn't been boring."

"I like boring!" I said. "I absolutely would prefer boring. Staying at home drinking my coffee and not having to run all over the place just to stay alive. Give me boring any day over this."

"I'm afraid that ship has sailed," Monty said. "Your life may contain moments of calm, short moments, mind you, but it will never be boring."

"Tell me something I don't know."

"We have to trust my uncle," he said, pulling on his sleeves. "One of the reasons the mages were successful during the war was due to him. In addition to being a formidable mage, he is a master tactician."

"I do trust him," I said as we climbed the stairs. "I just want a few normal days. Is that too much to ask?"

"There's no such thing as normal," Monty said, with a small smile as he looked up the stairs. "Not for us. The most we can hope for is the calm before the storm, and it appears we will experience many more storms. Ready?"

"Am I ever ready for this insanity?"

"Good," Monty said. "Let's go."

We raced up the remaining stairs.

TWENTY-TWO

We arrived at the top level just as an explosion rocked the entrance to the Brooklyn Battery Tunnel on the Manhattan side.

"Seems like Emeric is on his way," I said. "Tell me again why Braun didn't crush him into magistrate paste? Would've made this whole situation easier to deal with."

"The Midnight Echelon is not supposed to be involved in human affairs," Monty said, looking toward the plume of smoke that rose from the entrance. "The fact that they assist us is due to some pact my uncle has with them or their leader."

"Dex is tight with Freya and Odin?" I asked in disbelief. "No way."

"That being said, you will notice they have only helped us in very specific situations and only in a limited capacity."

"They didn't seem so limited on Little Island against Gault," I said. "I do see what you're saying, though. If they go on a rampage, it may cause friction with the other pantheons."

"Similar to how Hades has been acting behind the scenes, indirectly influencing events, but never taking direct action."

"Except against Tartarsauce," I said. "He got directly involved there."

"They forced his hand by taking Persephone," Monty clarified. "I daresay he could have done more if he had wanted to."

I recalled watching Hades in action as he fought against Tartarus and his minions. Hades easily held his own against an old god.

"I doubt Emeric will enhance himself or his minions," Monty continued, looking at his watch, then toward Governor's Island and the large fort that was easily visible from where we stood. "We have close to twenty minutes before he arrives downstairs at the SMDC, then at least another ten before he reaches the walkway provided the group is sizable."

"That gives us thirty minutes until contact," I said, still focused on the smoke rising. "Where am I waiting?"

"Over there," Monty said, pointing to the far end of the walkway. "It should take us five minutes to get there."

"That leaves you twenty-five minutes," I said. "Will that give you enough time to activate the Stronghold runes?"

"Not much choice in the matter," Monty said. "I'll have to make it work. I need a signal from you when you're falling back to the fort, something clear and unmistakable."

"Like my screams of panic as I evade Emeric and his Sanitizers?"

"Something a little less dramatic," he said. "Something only you can do."

"I'll fire a magic missile into the air, you won't be able to miss that."

Monty nodded.

"That should work," he said. "Once you release your signal, you must head to the fort, bringing Emeric with you.

Once he and his minions are on the island, I'll activate the Stronghold defenses. The ley-lines will create a defensive perimeter preventing egress and the runes will neutralize the entire island."

"We'll be trapped on the island."

"Yes."

"You won't be able to cast."

"Nor will any other mage," he said. "I still have my Sorrows and you have Ebonsoul."

"I'm sure Emeric will have weapons too."

"He doesn't have an *Aspis* or a hellhound on his side," Monty said. "I'd say in that scenario, we have the clear advantage."

"I wish I felt as confident as you sound."

We headed off to the far end of the walkway.

"How are you feeling?" Monty asked when we reached the end of the walkway. "Still feeling energized?"

"Somewhat," I said, focusing on my body for a few seconds. "It's beginning to wear off. Is there a crash afterward? Will I feel like I need a nap after it wears off?"

"No," Monty said, shaking his head. "Make sure you're on the far end of the walkway, as far from the ventilation tower as possible."

"What are you going to do?"

"Give you some assistance getting Emeric on the island," Monty said. "There is a chance he may hesitate in his pursuit if he feels it's a trap. He may be an insufferable boor, but he's still a magistrate. He's not stupid and will be looking for some kind of deception. I will provide him some incentive to give chase."

"How are you going to do that from the fort?"

"Leave that to me," Monty said, holding up the book. "Just stay on the far end and get him to come to you. We need him on the island when I activate the defenses."

"I'll do my best," I said. "You better get going."

"Simon do not engage him until the defenses are up," Monty said, resting a hand on my shoulder. "His acid orbs are—"

"I know," I said, looking up at the brightening sky. "I'm not looking to get melted today. We'll have a chat until the defenses are up. Then we'll have a *conversation* about his redecorating our home."

"Use your defenses," he said. "I'll see you at the fort."

I nodded and he took off at a dead run.

"Guess he was still energized too," I said mostly to myself and Peaches who sat by my side. "Let's go, boy."

We ran to the far end of the walkway.

When we reached the end, I formed a dawnward, stepped in front of it, and waited.

I didn't have to wait long.

"Shit," I muttered under my breath. "They're early."

Braun must have been feeling nice.

A large group of Sanitizers spilled out of the ventilation tower onto the surrounding platform. I really hoped Monty would be able to find the on switch to the Stronghold defenses in a hurry, or else this was going to be a short, painful battle.

Mixed in with the Sanitizers, I saw about a dozen Verity agents, in their impeccable black mageiform suits and looking out of place with the Grand Council Sanitizers.

I couldn't see their expressions, they were still too far away, but I knew when Emeric arrived. The crowd of Sanitizers parted and made room for the magistrate to step onto the concrete platform encircling the tower.

The walkway itself had been built on a makeshift pier of stones. To either side of the walkway, I could see the stones the walkway rested on. Beyond the stones were the waters of Diamond Reef.

I didn't need to see his face to know he had gone through a rough night.

The walkway was a perfect funnel for holding off a larger force, as long as that larger force didn't want to go for a swim. I was counting on them staying on the walkway at least for the time being.

I had a feeling that was going to change soon.

Emeric began crossing the walkway.

Behind him, like the good little soldiers they were, followed the Sanitizers. Behind them, demonstrating the hierarchy at play, followed the Verity agents.

Emeric stopped about halfway across the walkway and peered across at me with an obvious look of disgust. Then he looked left and right, before returning his gaze to me.

Unlike the rest of the mages behind him, Emeric appeared as if he had just stepped off a Paris runway. His suit was immaculate and pressed. Everything was perfect, not a hair was out of place.

The illusion stopped at his face.

I could see the small cuts and bruises, and as I looked carefully, I noticed he had crossed the walkway with a slight wince every time he stepped on his left foot. He approached slowly and was doing his best to hide the limp.

Braun must have given him a solid beating.

"Magistrate," I said with a short nod and a smile. "You made it, welcome."

Peaches, who sat next to me, let out a low growl. Emeric glanced across the walkway at him and took half a step back.

The disgust on his face quickly turned to anger. He took a moment to compose himself before addressing me. Mages and their egos; it was almost too easy.

"Where is Mage Montague?"

"He asked me to wait for you," I said, stepping into button pushing mode. "He said something about a lowly magistrate was no match for him. He would wait for a real challenge and face the Emissary, and that I could handle you."

"Handle me?" Emeric repeated as his face became red. "You? Could handle me? You're not even—"

"I know, I know," I said quickly putting up a hand and making all the mages behind Emeric flinch. "I told him as much, but he insisted. Said you were a coward for running away at the Abyss. I think he said—one second, I want to get this right—'a real mage would have stood and faced Grey, but you're just a lapdog who nips at the Emissary's heels.'"

His face was turning a bright shade of red now.

"He said what?"

"No self-respecting magistrate, not a real one at least, would let others fight his battles for him while remaining behind," I said. "A real magistrate leads the way in battle. Sort of like what you're doing now. Leading the way for your men. Well done."

Emeric formed two large black orbs, one in each hand. They crackled with so much energy I could hear them sizzle from where I stood. Getting hit by either of them would be the start of a bad week.

"Did he say *anything* else?"

It was time to send him over the edge.

"Plenty," I said. "He called the Emissary a pretender. Something about the Dubois family being illegitimate. How it was always the Montagues who directed and led the magical community."

"Lies," Emeric seethed. "He lies."

At this point, I was just making things up, I didn't really know the entire history of the Montagues or the Dubois families, but I did know that Emeric had placed the Emissary on a pedestal. Attacking him was ten times worse than attacking Emeric.

"Did you know," I continued. "That Alain, you don't mind

if I call him Alain, do you? Anyway, little Alain used to cheat on his magical tests? Crazy, right? It was Mage Montague who gave him the answers way back when they were still students. I heard Alain is as dumb as a rock."

I thought I could see the magistrate visibly tremble with rage.

"*Emissary* Dubois was an exemplary student and mage," Emeric growled, clenching his fists. "He is without peer. It is why the Grand Council chose him as the youngest Emissary in the history of the Council."

That was the issue with idol-worship, it made you weak and vulnerable. It exposed your pain points to your enemies if they knew how to exploit them.

I knew.

I shook my head. I was going to have to run after my next few statements. I started backing up slowly.

"I don't know, from what I heard, without Mage Montague, Alain Dubois would be nothing, less than nothing. The Grand Council wouldn't have noticed him."

Those last sentences may have been a little much, since the red in his face deepened and I could tell his breath caught as he tried to form his next words.

For a brief moment, the real concern of my words getting me killed crossed my mind. I swatted the concern away and smiled at Emeric with a shrug.

"That's why I'm here," I said. "To handle you."

"Surrender."

"You mean you wish to surrender to me? Very well, I accept."

"You are a fool, a dead fool," Emeric seethed. "I will destroy Mage Montague with my own hands, but first, you will die."

I patted Peaches on his ginormous head.

<*Time to go, boy. Stay close to me and do not bite them.*>

<Not even a small bite?>

<No, we need to get to Monty. Stay close to me.>

I took a few steps forward, still feeling energized from Monty's energy cast, pivoted on my front foot and ran in the opposite direction, right toward my dawnward.

Emeric unleashed his orbs at me.

TWENTY-THREE

I heard the crackling orbs behind me right before I crossed the dawnward.

I dove forward and rolled through the dawnward, not breaking my stride as I powered through the violet dome of energy. Peaches had blinked out and was ahead of me as I ran.

The acid orbs smashed into my dawnward.

I glanced behind me and made a mental note. My dawnward had limited effectiveness against Emeric's orbs, but it did manage to hold them back, even if it was only for a few seconds.

I could do plenty with a few seconds of breathing room.

I was off the walkway and on Governor's Island in under a minute, I made sure to run fast, but not so fast that they would lose me. They kept pace, chasing me.

The property around the fort was made up of small homes, other buildings and plenty of trees. There were some industrial sites and plenty of small roads that led to and from the fort.

Governor's Island may have no longer been a mage

Stronghold, but it did get plenty of visitors every year. In addition, some people actually lived on the island.

Emeric ran right behind me, but his Sanitizers were pulling their flanking maneuvers while the Verity agents were bringing up the rear. It was a coordinated attack. Had I the time to admire the tactic, I would have been impressed.

After a few minutes of this, I heard Emeric call out.

"Hold!" he said as he and his minions stopped. "Strong, you have nowhere to run. We're on an island, do you intend to swim back to the city?"

I stopped and turned.

He was a lot closer than I would've preferred, which meant that the energy from Monty's cast was either wearing off or had completely worn off and I was running on adrenaline and fear.

"I'm a strong swimmer," I said. "I could probably make it."

"Why die with the Montagues?" Emeric asked as the Sanitizers spread out. "Reconsider your options."

They were good.

By Emeric stopping, and them fanning out, they were trying to cut off my only path of escape.

A few more minutes and it would work.

I slowly kept backing up, keeping an eye on Emeric and letting my senses keep track of his Sanitizers.

"Reconsider my options?" I said. "What? A quick death or a slow one? Pass on both, thanks."

"This is no life," Emeric said, "running for your life like some hunted animal. I can put in a word with the Emissary. You're not a mage, it can work in your favor, and garner you leniency. The Emissary is a fair and just man."

"I can tell," I said, glancing around. "What is this, thirty against one? Feels pretty fair."

Emeric looked around at his men and motioned for them to stop. They stood still, focused on me.

"You don't realize this is over," Emeric said. "I don't want to kill you, but you're making it difficult to spare your life."

"Oh? This is you sparing my life?" I asked. "I didn't realize. It looks more like someone trying to end my life."

"You misunderstand, Strong," he said. "None of this concerns you."

"Sure seems like it does, unless you and your men are chasing someone else?" I said, glancing behind me. "I'm not seeing anyone else, so I'm guessing I'm the one being chased."

He sighed and shook his head.

"This is futile."

"What is?" I asked. He was acting entirely too comfortable and it was giving me a bad gut feeling. Something was off. "What is futile?"

"This plan of yours, it's flawed," he said, extending his arms. "Mage Montague isn't powerful enough on his own to activate the Stronghold runes. They have been dormant for decades."

My face must have given something away because he smiled and nodded.

"You didn't think we would know about this place?" he asked. "We are the Grand Council. We know everything. The runes will not activate, the ley-line perimeter defense will fail, and Mage Montague will die here, and you along with him, if you do not desist from this path."

"You're wrong."

"You know I speak the truth," he said. "Even now, the Emissary is on his way here. He will be here within the hour. Mage Montague is doomed, as is his uncle."

"You can't," I said. "Mage Montague is innocent."

His face transformed into a mask of rage for a brief moment.

"No one is innocent, no one," he spat. "Mage Montague turned his back on the magical community. He has been a rogue mage for far longer than you have known him."

"You don't know him."

"It is you who does not know him," he said softening his voice, to get me to drop my guard. "He has never shown you his true self."

"He's my friend, my brother."

"He is no such thing," he said, his voice sharp again. "He only cares for himself. Do you not see? He left you alone to face me, a magistrate. Would a friend do that? Would a brother expose you to such danger?"

"You don't know him."

"I *do* know him," he said. "You do not need to join him in this folly. You have a life to live, you are still young. Do not throw your life away."

"How did you know?" I asked. "About this place?"

"Once we declared you outcasts, we knew Dexter would try to force a confrontation," he said. "This was the most logical place to do so. We made sure the Stronghold runes were disabled, and I was sent to capture you both, but you are not the true target."

"Dex," I said as it dawned on me. "This was all to capture *Dex?*"

"Mage Tristan Montague is a promising mage," Emeric said with a nod. "In a few shifts, he will become an Archmage. The pride of the Montagues."

"You're trying to prevent that from happening."

"Not trying, we are succeeding," he said. "Tristan Montague is the son Dexter never had. He will do everything, anything to keep him safe. Tristan is collectively Dexter's greatest strength and his greatest weakness, as all children are to their parents."

"What are you saying?"

"We will capture Tristan Montague, and once Dexter arrives to rescue his family, the Stronghold runes *will* be activated, rendering the entire island a null zone. Dexter will surrender to keep Tristan alive, but he will fail."

"You're going to kill them."

"Yes," he said, his voice cold. "This branch of the Montague line ends today. Dexter and Tristan will both meet their demise on this island. The Emissary will see to it."

"The Emissary won't be able to cast if you activate the Stronghold runes," I said. "No mage will."

"There are many ways to kill an enemy that do not require casting," he said. "Now, you can avoid all this."

"What are you talking about?"

"We are not here for you, Strong, you know this," he said, stepping forward slowly. "We are here for Mage Montague. You can walk away from all this, go back to your old life as a detective, helping out your friend in the NYTF—Ramirez was it?"

He had done his homework.

I narrowed my eyes at him and felt that he was spooling energy as he walked. He was better than I anticipated. He had accumulated enough energy to blast me across the island with his next orb, if it didn't melt me first.

"We are men of action, Magistrate, lies do not become us," I said. "You threaten my family and expect me to walk away? I'm going to end you and your Emissary."

"You are making a mistake, one you won't realize until it's too late," he said. "Goodbye, Simon Strong."

I drew Grim Whisper, dropped two of the closest Sanitizers and turned to run. I felt the surge of power behind me spike as he unleashed an orb.

He was close...too close.

I gathered my energy and hoped that Monty was ready because I was coming in acid-hot. I focused the energy within and extended my arm.

"Ignis vitae!" I yelled.

I unleashed a violet beam of energy into the sky as I ran through the property outside the fort.

The large orb of energy behind me punched through some trees and demolished a small house as it headed for me.

"You should have fired that pathetic beam at me," Emeric called out from behind me. "At least you would have gone down fighting like a man, not running like the dirty mongrel you are."

I really hated this magistrate.

I ran around a few more structures. The orb punched its way through each one of them, not even slowing down to give me hope.

In the distance, I saw the entrance to Fort Jay.

I wasn't going to make it.

Around me, I sensed the Sanitizers. Some of them were getting orbs of their own ready.

"Don't waste your energy," Emeric called out. "He won't outrun the seeker, it's keyed to his energy signature. He's a dead man running. Leave him and search the fort for Mage Montague. He will be in the defensive control tower."

The Sanitizers peeled off, and in seconds, I was alone.

Except for the seeker still chasing me.

It was getting closer as I approached the large stone archway which made up the entrance to Fort Jay. But first, I had to cross a small foot-bridge that led to the main archway.

I could hear the crackling behind me as the orb closed in.

I was about to turn and fire a magic missile into Emeric's acid orb when I was shoved violently to the side and forced to eat several inches of grass as I slid across the grass-filled moat.

"What the—?" I managed as I saw my hellhound slam his head into the acid orb. "Peaches! No!"

He hit it so hard that the acid orb crashed into several nearby Sanitizers, sanitizing them from this life, as it melted them on impact. I didn't understand how he managed not to get melted himself, but I was too shocked to argue.

The next moment, I heard the crack of lightning followed by a deep rumble of thunder. A massive wave of energy raced across the island and I felt the steady thrum of ley-line power hover in the air around me.

Monty had activated the Stronghold runes.

I rolled to my feet as Peaches bounded toward another group of Sanitizers.

<*They're dangerous! Stop!*>

<*They're not dangerous now. Not for me. Can I bite them?*>

<*Bite but don't chew and they're still dangerous. Don't let them hurt you.*>

<*They can't hurt me, if they can't see me.*>

He bounded away and blinked out.

He reappeared seconds later and chomped on a Sanitizer who managed to scream in surprise before Peaches clamped onto his arm and flung him into a nearby tree.

The Sanitizer was unconscious before he hit the ground.

Peaches blinked out again pursuing Emeric's minions.

They didn't stand a chance.

I crossed over the foot bridge and under the archway entrance into an open clearing—the main courtyard. In the center, stood Emeric holding a black blade, facing a ragged looking Monty.

His suit was torn on one side and I could see what looked like burn marks along one side of his face. Whatever he had done to activate the Stronghold defenses, it had taken it out of him. There was no way he could face Emeric in his condition.

"You managed to activate the defenses, but it won't save you Montague," Emeric said. "I don't need my abilities to dispose of you. Magistrates of the Grand Council are trained to fight with and without their abilities, you know this."

"I also know the Grand Council mages have grown complacent," Monty said, holding one of his Sorrows. "You depend on your abilities more and more with each passing year. When was the last time you held a blade in your hand?"

"I prepare for every eventuality, including defeating an enemy without my abilities," Emeric answered, hefting his blade. "Can you say the same?"

I walked over and stood by Monty.

"You look like hell," I said under my breath. "Are we really doing this?"

"The Emissary is on his way," Monty said. "They rigged the defenses to detonate the control tower if tampered with."

"Let me guess, you tampered with it."

He held up half of a scorched book.

"You could say that," he said. "Cascade reaction was faster than I expected. Only managed one of my blades, but the key worked."

"We're locked in," I said. "Peaches is out there munching on his men and all we have to do is take down a magistrate. How hard can this be?"

Monty stared at me as Emeric removed his jacket.

"It's to be both of you, then," Emeric said, stepping into a fighting stance and holding his sword by his side. "I will lay your cold bodies out for the Emissary to inspect when he arrives. Then we will dispose of Dexter when he gets here to rescue you."

"Don't reveal anything until you have a real opening," Monty said, keeping his eyes on the magistrate. "Gather your energy. You won't get a second chance."

I nodded.

"We fight as one," I said, glancing at Monty. "Can you fight?"

"I'm not dying on this island today."

"I'll take that as a yes," I said and formed Ebonsoul. "Let's take him down."

TWENTY-FOUR

I drew Grim Whisper to fire into his chest and end this quickly.

Emeric had other plans.

He closed the distance between us in an instant.

He led with his elbow into my chest, striking my right pectoral with an explosive blow. It sent a jolt of pain down my right arm, loosening my grip on my gun, which he proceeded to strip from my hand with a downward strike on my wrist.

I watched Grim Whisper sail off to the side, as Emeric thrust forward with his blade. Monty parried the thrust aimed for my chest, and received a fist to his jaw for saving me from getting skewered.

I slashed at Emeric's thigh as Monty rolled with the blow and recovered. He spit out blood as he gathered himself.

We both stepped back and circled the magistrate.

"Is this the best you can do?" Emeric taunted. "Pathetic."

I stepped forward, but Monty placed a hand on my shoulder.

"As one," Monty said. "I will create the opening. Don't miss."

We closed in on Emeric, attacking at the same time.

Emeric wasn't just a skilled swordsman, he was exceptional. He dodged our attacks, parried our cuts, and redirected thrusts with ease. Several times, I nearly cut Monty as Emeric pivoted or parried my attack.

Monty stepped in closer and began pressing his attack. He gave me a look that I knew meant, get ready. Monty closed the distance as Emeric gave ground. I kept close but I didn't dare jump into the blender that their attacks had become.

This was no longer Monty and me fighting Emeric.

It was Monty rising to Emeric's level and making him work for every parry or dodge. Emeric lost his smug look of superiority and flexed the muscles of his jaw.

He was now fighting for his life.

They both were.

Their blades moved faster than I could anticipate. I needed to stay close, but not so close that either one would cut me.

"You would have made an excellent magistrate, if your uncle hadn't betrayed the Grand Council," Emeric said, pressing an attack. "He should have joined us. Instead he killed you both."

"Why would I settle for less by joining the Grand Council?" Monty asked parrying and then sidestepping a series of slashes from Emeric. "You and your kind corrupt everything you touch."

"Narrow-minded to the end," Emeric said. "Mages of your kind must be purged. We don't live in your idealistic fantasies. We live in reality. Life is not fair or just. It is what we make of it."

Emeric pushed forward and Monty stumbled back, glancing at me as he did so. In that same moment, Emeric produced a long dagger and drove it into Monty's thigh.

No, Monty tell me this isn't the opening you created.

As he stumbled back, Emeric scored a slash along Monty's sword arm, causing him to lose his blade. Monty fell to one knee as Emeric raised his blade.

"I should have expected the deception," Monty said his voice thick with pain. "Typical of the Grand Council."

"Yes, you should have," Emeric said, shaking his head. "You expected honor where there was none. Fairness where only one rule exists—survival. Typical Montague."

He started to bring down his sword, aimed at Monty's neck.

"*Mors Ignis,*" I whispered and placed my hand against Emeric's chest. "You should've been paying more attention."

A blast of darkflame exploded from my hand and into Emeric's chest, shoving him away from Monty several feet as he brought his sword down, narrowly missing Monty's neck. Dark violet trails of energy raced inside his body.

I stepped back, unsure of what I had just done.

"How?" Emeric said, stumbling back and falling as he looked down at his body in disbelief. "You're nothing, an insignificant afterthought. What did you do? Impossible." Real fear crossed Emeric's face. "The island has been neutralized, how did you—?"

"Simon," Monty said. "My sword, hurry. We must move."

"I don't understand," I said, grabbing Monty's sword and getting him to his feet. "What happened?"

"Move, now," Monty said pointing forward. "The archway."

We ran to the archway as Emeric convulsed on the ground.

"What's happening to him?" I asked taking a step toward Emeric. "My magic missile has never done that before."

Monty grabbed me by the arm and pulled me back before collapsing against the wall.

"Dawn...dawnward, now," Monty rasped. "Or we'll join him. Hurry."

I cast a dawnward.

The violet dome of energy filled the archway as we moved to the farthest end of the entrance. A few seconds later, Emeric exploded in dark violet and black flame, taking out most of the courtyard with him.

When we could see clearly, sections of the archway were missing. The road all around the courtyard was destroyed. What used to be the courtyard looked like the aftermath of a major missile strike.

"What the hell just happened, Monty?"

"Control tower," he said looking pale. "No time. We need to get to the control tower before...before the Emissary gets here."

"What are we going to do at the control tower?"

"Activate...activate circle," he said. "Escape."

"What do you mean?" I asked "He won't be a threat; he'll be neutralized once he gets here."

"No, the defenses are failing," Monty said. "I can reroute power to the SMDC circle from the control tower."

"That circle won't work, you said so yourself, it's missing a piece."

Monty reached into a pocket and handed me a long piece of copper.

"The catalyst," I said, looking at the piece of copper. "You found it?"

He nodded.

"These defenses will fall before he arrives," Monty said. "They've been out of commission for too long without regular upkeep. I had to localize the neutralization here, to the courtyard."

"What are you saying?"

"They damaged the Stronghold defenses beyond repair,"

he said. "If I can reroute the power, we can get off the island before the Grand Council reinforcements arrive with the Emissary."

"You have a dagger in your leg and you've lost too much blood," I said. "You can't move. Can you use your ability?"

"Not yet," he said. He was getting paler by the second and the panic in the back of my mind was racing to the front. "Keeping you alive is the priority, not the circle."

"You don't understand, once the Emissary gets here, he *will* kill us," he said. "I can't face him in this condition."

"We barely survived Emeric *without* his abilities," I said. "We can't face him at all."

"Get me to the control tower," he said, trying to stand. "I can delay the Emissary and give you time to get to the SMDC."

"You're insane if you think I'm leaving you here alone to face the Emissary," I said. "We all go or none of us do."

"Don't be foolish, Simon," he said. "It serves no one for all of us to die here."

I felt the charged sensation in the air drop around us and disappear. The Stronghold defenses were failing fast.

"Ley-lines are down," Monty said looking out of the entrance. "The runes will be next. You need to get off the island before then."

"You can't move in this condition," I said. "You need to be healed. Emeric said the Emissary would be here within the hour. We have time."

"Not enough, and your healing ability is not up to this level," he said. "You would need to know extensive—"

"Stop talking."

<*Boy! I need you here now! Monty is hurt!*>

Peaches appeared next to me a few seconds later.

<*The angry man is hurt. My saliva can heal him.*>

<*I know. You need to slap him with your tongue. Do it.*>

"He needs to use his saliva on you," I said looking at Monty. "It's the only way."

"This is a Zegna," Monty said looking down at his trashed suit. "You want me to let your creature salivate all over it?"

"Unless you want to be buried in it, yes. Your call."

He closed his eyes and nodded his head.

"Fine, but I'm not going to enjoy this."

"You don't need to enjoy it," I said. "Just tolerate it long enough until you can heal yourself and get us off this island."

He nodded without opening his eyes.

"Do it, boy."

Peaches slapped Monty with his tongue several times, thoroughly dousing him in hellhound saliva. By the time Monty pushed him off, his hair, shirt, and jacket collar were completely soaked.

I did my best not to smile as Monty got to his feet.

"Can you cast?" I asked, as Peaches shook his head spreading more saliva around the archway. "Are you healed enough?"

"Almost, which is good and bad news since it means the defenses will be gone when the Emissary arrives," he said, taking hold of the dagger in his leg. "However it does mean I can do this."

He gestured as he removed the dagger from his leg. The wound filled with golden light as it closed without spilling blood.

"That worked," I said. "You'll be able to heal yourself soon."

"Not that it will matter, since you will all be dead," a voice said from behind us. "You *will* suffer for killing my magistrate."

"Emissary?" I said under my breath without turning.

Monty nodded as we both turned to face our enemy.

The Emissary was dressed in an upscale version of a black

magistrate suit. I could see softly glowing golden runes flowing over the fabric. His tall frame filled most of the archway and his dark eyes blazed with a contained rage.

His cream-colored shirt was accentuated with a gold-colored tie, both of which were also rune-covered. He radiated power and if I had any doubt about the Stronghold defenses no longer working, they were gone in that instant.

"Emissary," Monty said. "Allow me to extend my deepest condo—"

The Emissary waved a hand and Monty was launched out of the archway and into the air above the courtyard. It had happened so fast, I barely caught it. One moment Monty was standing beside me, the next he wasn't.

"I told you, I would make you suffer," the Emissary said, looking up into the sky where Monty was still climbing. "I think I'll start by breaking all your bones. I'm sure Dexter will enjoy seeing what's left of you. What do you think, *Aspis?*"

"I think you better bring him down in one piece," I said, drawing Ebonsoul. "If you know what's good for you."

"Is that a threat?"

"It's a promise," I said. "Bring him down, now."

"Oh, I will," the Emissary said. "With as much force as possible."

Peaches growled next to me and entered Emissary shred mode.

The Emissary ignored Peaches and gestured.

Monty stopped climbing and reversed direction. He was coming down faster, faster than should've been possible. It looked like the Emissary had increased gravity, or Monty's weight.

He wasn't going to just break his bones.

If Monty hit the ground at his current velocity he would

be dead on impact. I dashed forward and attempted to bury Ebonsoul in the Emissary's midsection.

I was met with a wall of force that crushed me against the wall.

"Let...him...go," I managed. "You fight like a cowar—"

"I want you to watch your friend, your *brother*, as he slams into the ground and breathes his last," he said, gesturing again as the force against my chest increased. "Then I'm going to increase the pressure you're feeling until your bones are reduced to dust."

"Don't...threaten me...with a good time."

He stared at me in disbelief.

"After that, I will deal with that upstart Dexter," he said. "Once he sees your destroyed bodies and realizes he has lost, it will destroy him. Then, I will give him the death he deserves."

"You mages really...like to hear the sound...of your own voice," I said, struggling against the pressure on my chest. "Why are you so scared of Dexter?"

He whirled on me and I realized Monty was coming down fast.

<*Boy, go grab Monty before he hits the ground!*>

Peaches blinked out next to me.

"That won't save him," the Emissary said. "Tristan is moving too fast. Even if your hellhound could latch onto him, which I highly doubt, all you have done is consign them both to a gruesome death. Now, watch."

He placed a finger under my chin and turned my face to look out into the courtyard. I struggled against him but lost as he turned my head.

With a flick of his finger, I felt the pressure on my face keep my eyes open. I wouldn't even be able to close my eyes.

"Wouldn't want you to miss a thing," he said with a smile. "It's not every day you get to lose your brother and your bondmate at the same time. I'd say this moment is historic. Wouldn't you?"

"Fu—"

"Let's not be crass," he said as the air left my lungs. "This is a special moment."

I was forced to look as Monty and Peaches raced to the ground. Right before they impacted, a green flash filled the courtyard.

Rage danced across the Emissary's face.

"I assume that wasn't you," he said, looking at me as he fought to control himself. "You have outlived your usefulness. Goodbye, Strong."

He stretched out his index finger, lowered his arm slightly, and punctured my heart. I felt the pressure keeping me pinned against the wall diminish as I slid down and fell to my knees, and then onto my side.

I faced the courtyard as the Emissary exited the archway and stepped into the devastation that used to be the courtyard.

I was dying.

Then my curse kicked into overdrive.

I heard Kali whisper in my ear.

This is not your time, my Marked One, not yet.

"On your feet, Deathless," a voice said behind me. "This is no time to be lying about. We have an Emissary to retire."

Dex.

I was still on my side and saw the Emissary slowly turn around.

"You're talking to corpses now, Dexter?" he said. "How sad to see such a mind deteriorate. How long has it been?"

"Not long enough," Dex said. "Alain, even though you tried to kill my kin, I'm going to offer you a way out. Use the Solitary Door."

"Your offer is for me to choose exile from this plane?

Forever?" Alain said with a laugh. "You think too much of yourself, Dexter. I am not a child to fall victim to your myths of being the Harbinger of Death."

"You decline my offer?"

"Completely," Alain said. "Come meet me in battle, if you dare."

"No," Dex said, nudging me with his foot. "Get your arse up or I will kick you into standing position, Deathless."

"That corpse isn't going—" Alain started as I got to my knees.

"No need for the threats, old man," I said with a few coughs. "He drove a finger into my heart, you know."

"What did you...what did you do?" Alain stammered. "I killed him."

"It doesn't stick with this one," Dex said, glancing at me and extending an arm, forming Nemain. "You did, however, upset his pup. He doesn't like it when people kill his bondmate, even if it is short-lived."

Monty and Peaches appeared behind us.

Dex reached back and handed Monty Nemain. Peaches let out a low growl as the runes along his flanks turned a bright red. I saw his eyes begin to glow.

We stepped out to the edge of the archway, standing on the stones in front of the destroyed courtyard. I looked around and felt power surge into my body.

Peaches came to stand next to me and suddenly grew several sizes larger. I felt my skin harden and saw his fur gleam with a metallic sheen.

Alain laughed.

"Come to your death, then!" he yelled, forming a bluish blade covered in black runes. "You face an Emissary of the Grand Council! Face me and tremble!"

"End him," Dex said. "He no longer wishes life, and so all we offer on this day is death."

TWENTY-FIVE

Peaches blinked out.

I raced forward as Peaches reappeared, slamming me up into the air, and away from the slash that would have cut me in half. I dropped down as Alain created a shield that Monty sliced to pieces instantly forcing the Emissary to jump out of the way.

Peaches blinked out and reappeared next to me as I landed on the ground and rolled to my feet.

"A hellhound battleform," Alain said with some fear in his voice. "You have no idea what you have unleashed. Dexter, this is madness. You know this battleform is a menace to all of humanity."

"You want to talk, now?" Dex said. "A shame that moment has passed. If you fear them so much, remove them from existence."

Alain paused and glanced at me and Peaches.

"I killed you once, I can do it again," he said. "Very well, their blood is on your hands, Dexter."

"I accept," Dex said. "Spill it, if you can."

Alain gestured and blue flames erupted around his sword.

"There will be no quarter given," Alain said.

"None asked," I answered. "Monty?"

"You have sought me out and you have found me," Monty said in a strange voice as he hefted Nemain. "Today, you rejected life. Today, I will be your final embrace."

I took a step back and *really* looked at the weapon he held.

It was Nemain.

Not the Nemain I was used to, if I could even describe it that way since I don't think I'd ever get used to the terror-inducing weapon.

No. This was Nemain as wielded by the Harbinger.

The weapon's two-foot handle was covered in glowing green runes, which matched the symbols along the oversized blade. The mace side, which formed the back of the deadly blade end, was a large semicircle of more rune-covered black steel with lethal spikes along the edge.

I only sensed death from Monty.

The power that came off the weapon beckoned to me promising the sweet dance of madness, glory, and the death of my enemies.

I looked at Dex, who gave me a grim nod.

I turned to Alain, and I almost pitied him.

"You should have chosen life," I said. "Peaches, go."

Alain sneered at me as Peaches blinked out.

He swung his sword, the blue flames trailing behind the blade, but nothing touched my hellhound. Harbinger Monty stepped in and swung Nemain. Alain was good. Better than good, probably one of the best.

He recovered from his missed swing against Peaches, slid to the side, and intercepted Nemain.

That was a mistake.

Nemain didn't even slow down.

It sliced through Alain's blade as if it wasn't even there. His blade shattered into several pieces as blue flames exploded all around us.

The Emissary siphoned the blue flames around us into his hands, forming a large flaming orb, which he unleashed at Monty.

Monty turned Nemain so that the flat of the blade caught the orb. It slammed into Nemain, pushing Monty back several feet. When the orb diminished, I saw Monty look at Alain over Nemain.

That's when I saw the Emissary show real fear.

"What are you?" he asked as Monty closed in on him. "What *are* you?"

"I am the Harbinger," Monty said. "You chose me, called me by name. Here I am."

The Emissary stepped back and fired a barrage of black orbs at Monty. They all bounced off Nemain harmlessly. Peaches blinked back in and fired a baleful glare at Monty who deflected the beam into the Emissary, launching him back.

Peaches blinked out again and reappeared a dozen feet above the Emissary where he hovered for half a second before he plummeted to the ground.

The Emissary recovered from the baleful glare reflection play in time to avoid a super dense Peaches landing on his chest.

Peaches cratered the ground and blinked out again.

I closed in on the Emissary.

I needed to end this before 'Harbinger Monty' or my 'very angry at being dropped from an insane height' hellhound ended up crushing the Emissary.

I focused the energy in my body as I stepped close.

Peaches blinked in and attempted to crash head-first into the Emissary. He narrowly dodged that attack only to face down a determined Harbinger Monty intent on bisecting him in half.

He managed to backpedal away from Monty and straight into me.

"*Mors Ignis*," I whispered, grabbing his wrist as darkflame engulfed the Emissary. "*Exuro*."

The darkflame exploded, increasing in intensity as the Emissary screamed. It didn't last more than a few seconds. When the flames died down, the Emissary was gone.

Only dust remained.

Dex walked up to Monty and removed Nemain from his hands. He walked past me, placing a hand on my shoulder before he made his way to the remains of the Emissary.

With a gesture, he removed the dust that used to be Emissary Alain Dubois.

"We need to go," Dex said his voice grim. "Now."

I opened my mouth to say something and he cut me down with a look.

"No questions, no words," he said, his voice a blade that cut through the silence of the courtyard. "We leave now, we speak later."

Monty and I both nodded.

Peaches blinked back in and came to my side.

Dex formed a large green teleportation circle.

In the distance, I could see the Grand Council reinforcements arriving on the island. If we stayed to fight, they would have to rename this place Death's Island.

We couldn't stay.

Dex stood next to me as he followed my gaze with his own.

"They would all die, wouldn't they?" I asked softly. "They wouldn't stand a chance."

"No, they wouldn't," Dex said solemnly. "That's why we

have to go. They think we are the enemy, but today we are saving the lives the Grand Council is willing to discard."

"This isn't over, is it?"

"For today, it is."

Dex gestured and Governor's Island disappeared in a green flash.

TWENTY-SIX

TWO DAYS LATER
MONTAGUE SCHOOL OF BATTLEMAGIC

"They won't let this go," Dex said. "They can't now."

"Are we really going to war with the Grand Council?" I asked. "Because that sounds senseless. Too many people will die because they believe everyone and anyone is expendable."

"We aren't going to war with them," Monty said. "We're going to end this war before it can even start."

"How exactly is that supposed to happen?" I said. "You saw the reinforcements on Governor's Island. They have more where that came from, not to mention all of Verity, the sects that still listen to them, the Dark Council, and any other groups they control or influence."

"Irrelevant," Monty said. "We are not engaging in direct warfare. We must employ guerrilla warfare. We must locate their headquarters and strike at the heart of the Grand Council."

"Good plan," Dex said. "Except no one knows where that

is. They move constantly and no one knows their locations. No one."

"I find that unlikely," Monty said. "Besides, I know where we can locate one of the best trackers in history."

"One of the best?" I asked. "Why wasn't he helping us before now?

"Because you weren't ready," Monty said. "I think you may be now, and it's she, not he."

"I wasn't ready?" I asked. "What do you mean she? Who is this person?"

"She will help you develop your skill as a shieldbearer," Monty said. "I will need assistance in increasing the potency of my casts"—he glanced at Dex—"without the use of Nemain. That weapon is dangerous. I don't know how you wield it."

"I don't," Dex said. "But I may have a solution to both your leveling-up problems."

"You do?" I asked. "Does this involve torture of some kind?"

"You could say that," Dex said with an evil smile. "You just have to finish your initiation."

"Initiation?" I asked slightly confused. "What initiation?"

"The Ten," Monty said. "You want us to join the Ten?"

"You're almost there," Dex said. "You just have to survive the rest of the initiation. From my understanding, you're going to go looking for Ichnaea, yes?"

"Yes," Monty said. "She can help us locate the Grand Council."

"She's not an easy goddess to find," he said. "In order for her to help you, you have to track and find her first."

"We're going to track a goddess?"

"Not just any goddess," Dex answered. "You're trying to locate the goddess of tracking. You think she's going to make it easy?"

"This is going to be impossible."

"Improbable," Monty said. "If we don't stop the Grand Council, there will be another war. Countless mages will die. Innocent mages. We can't let—"

"We're not going to let it happen," I said. "If that means finding Echinacea, then we will find her."

"I strongly suggest you learn her correct name before we meet her in person," Monty said. "Rumor has it she doesn't have much of a sense of humor."

"Wonderful," I said. "What are the chances she helps us?"

"If we manage to find her, high," Monty said. "That's our best chance at recruiting her assistance."

"Aye, if you can locate her, she will help you, but she has trials and I hear they are difficult," Dex said. "In the meantime I will convene a gathering of the Ten to discuss your initiation."

"Uncle, I have been wanting to know," Monty said his voice serious. "Are you a member of the Ten?"

"I can't say," Dex answered. "Not because I don't want to, but because I'm not allowed to, lad. Just know that the Ten and me, we are joined in more ways than one. I hope that will suffice for now. If you survive your initiation, I may be able to share more."

"If we survive?"

"Yes, but first, we have work to do," he said. "Take the next few days to rest up. For now, going home is not an option. The Grand Council will continue to hunt you. Best you stay here until we resolve this situation."

"How long will that be?" I asked. "Not that I'm in a hurry to fight for my life again."

"As long as needed," Dex said. "It may be time to pay your Underworld home a visit as well. I'm sure Hades may have some insights into Ichnaea's location, considering she's part of his pantheon."

"It would be a good start," Monty said. "In the meantime, we train."

"Train?" I asked. "What happened to taking a few days rest?"

"We will, right after we train on your dawnward and my casts," he said. "We also need to discuss this darkflame of yours. It seems too volatile."

"Aye," Dex said. "It may be best to investigate what happened on the island before moving ahead. Plenty of time for rest—later. Things cut a little close with the Emissary."

I nodded and had to agree.

We were definitely stepping into a level where power made the difference. The Emissary was able to stand his own against a battleform hellhound, his bondmate, and a Harbinger.

If that wasn't a different weight class, I didn't know what was. Dubois was only an Emissary; it stood to reason that the actual Grand Council was even stronger. We couldn't face them as we were now, we had to get stronger.

If that meant more training, that's what we would do.

I was not going to let another war start.

Not while I had the power to stop it.

Even if it meant living the rest of my life as an outcast.

It was a small price to pay for lasting peace.

THE END

AUTHOR NOTES

Thank you for reading this story and jumping into the world of Monty and Strong with me.

Disclaimer: The Author Notes are written at the very end of the writing process. This section is not seen by the ART or my amazing Jeditor. Any typos or errors following this disclaimer are mine and mine alone.

Let's be honest, Monty, Simon and the Mighty Peaches have been outcasts for some time.

It's true.

What changed in this book?

The Grand Council is taking out the hate and animosity they have toward Dex on MS&P. Why?

Because Dex doesn't have any apparent weaknesses, because he relocated an entire sect, and because he's staggeringly powerful and that has a tendency to bring out the worst in your enemies.

Also MS&P *are* his weakness.

The Grand Council can't mount a direct attack on Dex, but they can go after his family, blood and found.

Let's take a step back first.

If you're reading this, I want to express my deepest and humblest THANKS! Thank you for being part of this adventure. We are currently on book MS&P24.

Take a moment to pause and really absorb that.

This was supposed to be a trilogy—that was 21 books ago. We are now on book 24, and it never ceases to amaze me that we are this far along in this adventure!

I sincerely appreciate you reading this (and every story I write). It always boggles my mind when readers express parts of a particular book that has moved to some of the deeper recesses of my mind(read that as not fresh in my memory) but is crystal clear to my readers.

Okay let's jump into OUTCAST.

The hitters are getting heavy.

Seriously Heavy.

Without stepping into spoiler territory, Monty & Simon are realizing that the enemies they are facing have kicked it up a (few) notches. It's becoming clear that the Terrible Trio is going to need to get stronger and in a hurry, if they are going to be able to face against those who want them removed permanently.

In this story they realize they aren't alone, but those who would stand with them are forcing them to level up. To move in these new circles, they will have accept certain truths.

People want them dead.

They will have to take a hard torturous and lonely journey.

Not everyone they know will be able to join them on this journey.

In the upcoming stories (SHIELDBEARER), Monty & Simon will make their circles smaller in order to get stronger. There will be more interaction with other members of the

Ten and they will have to have an extensive conversation with Hades (the god not the place).

The battleform with Simon and Peaches will evolve, and things will get precarious as well as their bond becoming strained. Monty will revisit some old casts and face the temptation to reacquire certain forbidden casts to better defeat their enemies.

Chi and Roxanne will step up more prominently in the next stories. They will both be hunted in order to bring Monty & Simon back to their plane. The Grand Council fights dirty and no one is safe. If making them outcasts won't work, threatening who they care for will be the next step.

For The Grand Council, the ends justify the means and the end they seek is the death of the Montagues, starting with Dex.

They cheat, they fight dirty, and they don't care.

There's only one rule with The Grand Council: there are no rules.

I had a great time writing this story. It's always fun to bring in characters to make cameo appearances, though Grey and Koda will have their own story coming out later this year (DIVINE HELL).

The answer to the frequent question is YES, there will be more TK and LD and more of the TEN. YES their story is in the works, I need to settle on whether the TEN's story starts waaay in the past and then jumps through time, or remains in the past for now.

Decisions, decisions.

What else is currently happening?

STONE (John Kane 2) is being written and DEATH-DANCERS is about halfway complete as of this writing. There's also a very fun Patreon super-short story (THE BUREAU) that I can see becoming a novella at some point down the road.

If everything remains on track we'll have M&S 25 (SAINTS & MONKS) this year, some Night Warden, the third John Kane (MEND) and the second romantasy story (COLD FRONT) arriving later this year too.

Somewhere in there I'll try and fit in some sleep lol.

This next part I repeat often because I find it to be profoundly true. Please forgive me for stating it again and know that I mean it all.
You are totally amazing.

As always, I couldn't do this incredibly insane adventure without you, my amazing reader. You jump into these adventures with me, when I say "WHAT IF?" you say: "Hmmm what if indeed. Let's find out where that idea goes!"

For that, I humbly and deeply thank you.

As always, I consider myself deeply fortunate to have the most amazing readers that are willing to leap into these worlds with the same reckless abandon I have in writing them. You truly spoil me. Few writers I know have such incredible readers that make it possible to explore and try creating new worlds, and introduce different characters.

Thank you so much for joining me as we load up the extra thermos (better bring three or four of them—industrial-sized) filled with the delicious inky Death Wish Javambrosia, some of you can call shotgun, but a few of you are going to have to shove the enormous hellhound in the back of the Dark Goat over if you want a seat (bring sausage/pastrami-for a guaranteed seat!), as we strap in to jump into all sorts of adventures!

We have plans to thwart, people to rescue, and property to renovate!

There is so much I WANT to share with you that I can't yet (but I will soon). Again, I want you to know that this adventure is incredible, but it's made even more amazing by having you on it with me.

I humbly and deeply thank you.

In the immortal sage words of our resident Zen Hellhound Master...

Meat is Life!

gratias tibi ago

SUPPORT US

Patreon
The Magick Squad

Website/Newsletter
www.orlandoasanchez.com

JOIN US

Facebook
Montague & Strong Case Files

Youtube
Bitten Peaches Publishing Storyteller

Instagram
bittenpeaches

Email
orlando@orlandoasanchez.com

M&S World Store
Emandes

BITTEN PEACHES PUBLISHING

Thanks for Reading!
If you enjoyed this book, would you please **leave a review** at the site you purchased it from? It doesn't have to be long... just a line or two would be fantastic and it would really help me out.

Bitten Peaches Publishing offers more books and audiobooks
across various genres including: urban fantasy, science fiction, adventure, & mystery!

www.BittenPeachesPublishing.com

More books by Orlando A. Sanchez

Montague & Strong Detective Agency Novels
Tombyards & Butterflies•Full Moon Howl•Blood is Thicker•Silver Clouds Dirty Sky•Homecoming•Dragons & Demigods•Bullets & Blades•Hell Hath No Fury•Reaping Wind•The Golem•Dark Glass•Walking the

Razor•Requiem•Divine Intervention•Storm Blood•Revenant•Blood Lessons•Broken Magic•Lost Runes•Archmage•Entropy•Corpse Road•Immortal•Outcast

Montague & Strong Detective Agency Stories
No God is Safe•The Date•The War Mage•A Proper Hellhound•The Perfect Cup•Saving Mr. K

Night Warden Novels
Wander•ShadowStrut•Nocturne Melody

Rule of the Council
Blood Ascension•Blood Betrayal•Blood Rule

The Warriors of the Way
The Karashihan•The Spiritual Warriors•The Ascendants•The Fallen Warrior•The Warrior Ascendant•The Master Warrior

John Kane
The Deepest Cut•Blur

Sepia Blue
The Last Dance•Rise of the Night•Sisters•Nightmare•Nameless•Demon

Chronicles of the Modern Mystics
The Dark Flame•A Dream of Ashes

The Treadwell Supernatural Directive
The Stray Dogs•Shadow Queen•Endgame Tango

Brew & Chew Adventures
Hellhound Blues

Bangers & Mash
Bangers & Mash

Tales of the Gatekeepers
Bullet Ballet•The Way of Bug•Blood Bond

Division 13
The Operative•The Magekiller

Blackjack Chronicles
The Dread Warlock

The Assassin's Apprentice
The Birth of Death

Gideon Shepherd Thrillers
Sheepdog

DAMNED
Aftermath

Nyxia White
They Bite•They Rend•They Kill

Iker the Cleaner
Iker the Unseen•Daystrider•Nightwalker

Fate of the Darkmages
Fated Fury

Stay up to date with new releases!
Shop www.orlandoasanchez.com for more books and audiobooks!

ART SHREDDERS

I want to take a moment to extend a special thanks to the ART SHREDDERS.

No book is the work of one person. I am fortunate enough to have an amazing team of advance readers and shredders.

Thank you for giving of your time and keen eyes to provide notes, insights, answers to the questions, and corrections (dealing wonderfully with my extreme dreaded comma allergy). You help make every book and story go from good to great. Each and every one of you helped make this book fantastic, and I couldn't do this without each of you.

THANK YOU

ART SHREDDERS

Amber, Anne Morando, Audrey Cienki
   Bethany Showell, Beverly Collie
   Chris Christman II

Dawn McQueen Mortimer, Denise King, Diane Craig, Dolly, Donna Young Hatridge

Hal Bass

James Wheat, Jasmine Breeden, Jasmine Davis, Jeanette Auer, Jen Cooper, Joy Kiili, Julie Peckett

Karen Hollyhead

Larry Diaz Tushman, Laura Tallman I, Luann Zipp

Malcolm Robertson, Maryelaine Eckerle-Foster, Melissa Miller Paige Guido

RC Battels, Rohan Gandhy

Sondra Massey, Stacey Stein, Susie Johnson

Tami Cowles, Terri Adkisson

Vikki Brannagan

Wendy Schindler

PATREON SUPPORTERS

Exclusive short stories
Premium Access to works in progress
Free Ebooks for select tiers

Join here
The Magick Squad

THANK YOU

Alisha Harper, Amber Dawn Sessler, Angela Tapping, Anne Morando, Anthony Hudson, ASH, Ashley Britt

Brenda French

Carolyn J. Evans, Carrie O'Leary, Christopher Scoggins, Cindy Deporter, Connie Cleary, Cooper Walls, Craig Gill

Dan Bergemann, Dan Fong, Daniel Harkavy, David Mitchell,

Davis Johnson, Dawn Bender, Di Hara, Diane Garcia, Diane Jackson, Diane Kassmann, Dorothy Phillips

E.A., Elizabeth Varga, Enid Rodriguez, Eric Maldonado, Eve Bartlet, Ewan Mollison

Federica De Dominicis, Fluff Chick Productions, Fred Westfall

Gail Ketcham Hermann, Gary McVicar, Groove72

Ingrid Schijven

James Burns, James Wheat, Jasmine Breeden, Jasmine Davis, Jeffrey Juchau, JF, Jo Dungey, Joe Durham, John Fauver(*in memoriam*), Joy Kiili, Just Jeanette

Kathy Ringo, Krista Fox

Leona Jackson, Lisa Simpson, Lizzette Piltch

Malcolm Robertson, Marie Stein, Mark Morgan, Mark Price, Mary Beth Wright, MaryAnn Sims, Maureen McCallan, Mel Brown, Melissa Miller, Meri, Duncanson

Paige Guido, Patricia Pearson, Peter Griffin, Pete Peters

Ralph Kroll, Renee Penn, Rick Clapp, Robert Walters

Samantha Rense, Sara M Branson, Sara N Morgan, Sarah Sofianos, Sassy Bear, Sharon Elliott, Shelby, Sonyia Roy, Stacey Stein, Steven Huber, Susan Bowin, Susan Spry

Tami Cowles, Terri Adkisson, Tommy, Trish Brown

Valerie Jondahl, Van Nebedum

W S Dawkins, Wendy Schindler, Wicketbird

***

I want to extend a special note of gratitude to all of our
Patrons in
The Magick Squad.

Your generous support helps me to continue on this amazing
adventure called 'being an author'.
I deeply and truly appreciate each of you for your selfless act
of patronage.

You are all amazing beyond belief.

THANK YOU

ACKNOWLEDGMENTS

With each book, I realize that every time I learn something about this craft, it highlights so many things I still have to learn. Each book, each creative expression, has a large group of people behind it.

This book is no different.

Even though you see one name on the cover, it is with the knowledge that I am standing on the shoulders of the literary giants that informed my youth, and am supported by my generous readers who give of their time to jump into the adventures of my overactive imagination.

I would like to take a moment to express my most sincere thanks:

To Dolly: My wife and greatest support. You make all this possible each and every day. You keep me grounded when I get lost in the forest of ideas. Thank you for asking the right questions when needed, and listening intently when I go off on tangents. Thank you for who you are and the space you create—I love you.

To my Tribe: You are the reason I have stories to tell. You cannot possibly fathom how much and how deeply I love you all.

To Lee: Because you were the first audience I ever had. I love you, sis.

To the Logsdon Family: The words *thank you* are insufficient to describe the gratitude in my heart for each of you. JL, your support always demands I bring my best, my A-game, and produce the best story I can. Both you and Lorelei (my Uber Jeditor) and now, Audrey, are the reason I am where I am today. My thank you for the notes, challenges, corrections, advice, and laughter. Your patience is truly infinite. *Arigatogozaimasu*.

To Leslie: Thank you for the amazing notes. Your first time in the M&S World was fantastic! Thank you for the insights!

To The Montague & Strong Case Files Group—AKA The MoB (Mages of Badassery): When I wrote T&B there were fifty-five members in The MoB. As of this release, there are over one thousand five hundred members in the MoB. I am honored to be able to call you my MoB Family. Thank you for being part of this group and M&S.

You make this possible. **THANK YOU.**

To the ever-vigilant PACK: You help make the MoB...the MoB. Keeping it a safe place for us to share and just...be. Thank you for your selfless vigilance. You truly are the Sentries of Sanity.

Chris Christman II: A real-life technomancer who makes the **MoBTV LIVEvents +Kaffeeklatsch** on YouTube amazing. Thank you for your tireless work and wisdom. Everything is connected...you totally rock!

To the WTA—The Incorrigibles: JL, Ben Z., Eric QK., S.S., and Noah.

They sound like a bunch of badass misfits, because they are. My exposure to the deranged and deviant brain trust you all represent helped me be the author I am today. I have officially gone to the *dark side* thanks to all of you. I humbly give you my thanks, and...it's all your fault.

To my fellow Indie Authors: I want to thank each of you for creating a space where authors can feel listened to, and encouraged to continue on this path. A rising tide lifts all the ships indeed.

To The English Advisory: Aaron, Penny, Carrie, Davina, and all of the UK MoB. For all things English...thank you.

To DEATH WISH COFFEE: This book (and every book I write) has been fueled by generous amounts of the only coffee on the planet (and in space) strong enough to power my very twisted imagination. Is there any other coffee that can compare? I think not. DEATH WISH—thank you!

To Deranged Doctor Design: Kim, Darja, Tanja, Jovana, and Milo (Designer Extraordinaire).

If you've seen the covers of my books and been amazed, you can thank the very talented and gifted creative team at DDD. They take the rough ideas I give them, and produce incredible covers that continue to surprise and amaze me. Each time, I find myself striving to write a story worthy of the covers they produce. DDD, you embody professionalism and creativity. Thank you for the great service and spectacular covers. **YOU GUYS RULE!**

To you, the reader: I was always taught to save the best for last. I write these stories for **you**. Thank you for jumping down the rabbit holes of *what if?* with me. You are the reason I write the stories I do.

You keep reading...I'll keep writing.

Thank you for your support and encouragement.

SPECIAL MENTIONS

To Dolly: my rock, anchor, and inspiration. Thank you...always.

Larry & Tammy—The WOUF: Because even when you aren't there...you're there. And of course for the Deathane.

Orlando A. Sanchez
www.orlandoasanchez.com

Orlando has been writing ever since his teens when he was immersed in creating scenarios for playing Dungeons and Dragons with his friends every weekend.

The worlds of his books are urban settings with a twist of the paranormal lurking just behind the scenes and with generous doses of magic, martial arts, and mayhem.

He currently resides in Queens, NY with his wife and children.

<u>Thanks for Reading!</u>

If you enjoyed this book
Please leave a review & share!
(with everyone you know)

It would really help us out!